THE ABLATIVE CASE

THE ABLATIVE CASE

Ralph McInerny

Five Star • Waterville, Maine

Published in 2003 in conjunction with Tekno Books and Ed Gorman.

Set in 11 pt. Plantin by Elena Picard.

Printed in the United States on permanent paper.

Library of Congress Cataloging-in-Publication Data

McInerny, Ralph M.
    The ablative case / Ralph McInerny.
        p. cm.
    ISBN 0-7862-5234-0 (hc : alk. paper)
    ISBN 1-4104-0124-3 (sc : alk. paper)
        1. Kidnapping—Fiction.   2. Psychiatrists—Fiction.
    I. Title.
    PS3563.A31166A635 2003
    813'.54—dc21   2003043423

To Janet Hutchings

Love is not love which alters when it alteration finds
Or bends with the remover to remove . . .

—William Shakespeare

CONTENTS

Part 1

MS. TAKEN

1

The kidnapper called at 2:20 p.m. on Monday and was put on hold, his ear filling with the insipid Muzak meant to soothe the breast made savage by delay. Lyndon Johnson Community College, in externals at least an institution of higher learning, beneficiary of state and federal largess, was not, in the matter of its telephone system, up to the state of the art. This is why Blanche Wiggins's voice was heard by every caller unacquainted with a more particular internal number.

"LJCC, would you hold?"

And then the Muzak began.

The kidnapper stewed through the three minutes it took Blanche to get back to him and then made his announcement.

"We have Mavis Navrone. I will call back in exactly one half-hour . . ."

"To whom should I direct your call?" Blanche said, sucking a mint, one eye on the miniature television set that kept her *au courant* with the agonies and intimacies of her favorite soap, "Rising Gorge." This show had started as a Saturday night spoof of soaps, acquired a following, and now competed in daylight hours with the serials it was meant to mock. During the year Blanche had been watching, satire had slipped away and the show was now no more, and no less, a parody than the others.

"We have kidnapped Mavis Navrone . . ."

"What department is she in, please?"

"This is a kidnapping!"

"There is a Navrone M in financial aid, is that she?"

Five seconds ticked toward eternity. "Yes."

"I'll put you through."

2

In financial aid, Mavis Navrone picked up her phone to hear a husky voice announce that she had been kidnapped.

"Is that you, Dwayne?"

"We have Mavis Navrone in custody!"

"Oh, stop it."

"Goddam it, I'm serious."

On Mavis's narrow face a smile gave way to a frown. "Dwayne," she said in a fierce warning whisper.

"This isn't Dwayne. We have kidnapped Mavis Navrone! So shut your goddam mouth a minute and listen to instructions."

Mavis was angry now. "This is Mavis Navrone speaking and please watch your language."

She sat listening to the silence on the line. Was it Dwayne, after all? The joke was his style. But the silence went on and then there was a click as the phone went dead.

Honestly. But she was left in a state of some confusion, wanting to be a good sport, if that had indeed been Dwayne on the phone, but finding it difficult to regard the call as a practical joke. She picked up the phone and waited for Blanche to come on.

"That call you just put through to me? What did he say?"

"Hold a minute, will you, hon?"

Mavis hummed along with the Muzak, telling herself the caller had to be her husband. She had always hated practical jokers but Dwayne was different.

"What a day!" Blanche said. "You still there?"

"This is Mavis Navrone in financial aid. You just put a call through to me." Mavis shook her wrist to get her watch in view. "Five minutes ago."

"Yes."

"I wondered how the man asked for me."

But Blanche, whose head must echo with hundreds of voices, messages, requests, could not pick Mavis's caller from among them.

"I see in the book you're Navrone, M."

"That stands for Mavis."

Of course she had never met the college switchboard operator. Did she even know where she was located? Financial aid occupied the third floor of a building across the street from the main college edifice, a tall narrow building that still looked like the office building it had been designed to be. The college, product of the mad notion that everyone has a constitutional right to a higher education, was the fruit of a conspiracy hatched by the congressman in whose district the LJCC was located, the borough government and the representatives of the two major political parties. All had been made happy by the flood of federal and state money available to bring a college education to the disadvantaged. Costs were allegedly held down by putting existent real estate to this new and noble purpose. The previous owners of the land and buildings, often relatives of the public servants involved, were glad to do their richly recompensed bit for higher education. Putting together a faculty from the flotsam and jetsam of the profession had been no problem and there was a constant supply of scarcely literate applicants attracted chiefly by card ads mounted in subway cars.

The assumptions on which LJCC had been built no longer obtained (to borrow a phrase from Jerome Jarbro, head of financial aid and Mavis's boss). The money, federal, state and municipal, was drying up. Potential students seemed to have difficulty reading the advertisements the college placed in specialized papers around town. There was a proposal before the city council to substitute enrollment in LJCC for incarceration in the case of certain nonviolent crimes and it was hoped that this, together with the abandonment of all entrance requirements, would keep the college afloat until a better time.

"Did he have an accent?" Mavis asked the operator.

Mavis could understand Italian at family gatherings, but English was her only real language, and that in its standard versions. The jargon of applicants was often beyond her ken. Toward the end of the day it was easy to grow impatient with the interpreters who seemed dumber than the students whose answers they were translating.

"What do you mean by an accent?" Blanche's voice seemed to arise from the Mississippi delta, roll across the Deep South and arrive in Penn Station on the Chattanooga Choo Choo.

"Can you trace calls?"

"I can put you through to campus security."

Mavis declined and hung up. The sight of a member of campus security always made her want to call a cop. She spun in her chair, frowned at the screen of her computer and began randomly hitting keys as she thought. There were two possibilities: either it was serious or it was a practical joke. If it was serious it might be Raul the Puerto

Rican applicant who wore the sleeves of his tee shirt rolled to his armpits the better to display his tattoos. He had taken umbrage (Jerome Jarbro again) when Mavis corrected the way he filled out a form.

"You want male."

"What mail?"

"I mean sex."

Two gold teeth added variety to his smile. "Yeah?"

"You put your X in the wrong box."

Raul looked at the interpreter and said something in Spanish. The interpreter rose to go. Mavis objected. The nature of the misunderstanding became clear. Before it was over Jerome Jarbro had to intervene. As Raul went off to be helped by the supervisor himself, he gave Mavis another golden smile. She in turn, to her own utter amazement and disbelief, gave him the finger. She had no idea whence the gesture came. She had never made it before, every day of the week she was provoked far more than this and managed not to step out of character. Raul's smile faded, his eyelids drooped; Mavis had made an enemy.

On the other hand, if the call was a joke, it had to be Dwayne. She picked up her phone and dialed.

"Dwayne?"

"Mavis!"

"Yes," she said, waiting for a sign that would tell her he had done it.

"Where are you?"

"Where am I? I'm at work. Where else would I be? Did you think I'd been kidnapped?"

A pause. "Don't be silly."

3

Gloria Sheahan lay on the rear seat of a Jaguar; her hands tied behind her back and a plastic trash bag pulled over the upper half of her body. All she knew was that she was in an intermittently moving vehicle and had to go to the bathroom so bad she could cry.

She had been hurrying down the hallway on her way to the ladies' when this nightmare began. She had just passed a stairway door, relief was only a few steps away, when there was a hiss of compressed air, a slipping and sliding of leather soles on the polished floor, and dark descended as the bag was pulled over her head. She was pulled violently backward through the stairway door while someone began to hit her on the head with something soft and heavy. The scream she had begun when the lights went out died when they went out again. She came to with her hands tied behind her, lying on her side, in a vehicle that must be going cross-town and was missing every light.

She lay listening to the familiar sounds of traffic: complaining horns, a roar of motors, the ceaseless racket of passing automobiles and taxis and buses and delivery trucks. It was the all but inaudible background music to which she worked in the financial aid office of Lyndon Johnson Community College, it was the daily drama she witnessed going to and from work, witnessed but, as she now reflected, never really noticed. How many automobiles had she passed that had a woman trussed up in a plastic bag in the back seat and never saw what was happening? It might have happened every day. She had learned the limitations of a citizen's responsibilities in the modern megalopolis. She rode in every morning from New Rochelle and rode out again every night, silently thanking God she had survived another day. She had tried to pray in her present plight but it needed all the attention she could muster not to wet her pants.

She could not plead with her unknown persecutors because they had stuffed a handkerchief into her mouth, a handkerchief redolent of the cheap perfume favored by Mavis Navrone. What sounds she managed to make could not compete with the street racket and the angry roar the motor of the car made when it started from a dead stop and hurtled through what to Gloria at least was darkness, angrily hooting at slower vehicles, changing lanes, failing to make the next light to a chorus of curses from the front seat.

There were two voices at least, a whiny high-pitched male she took to be the driver, another more controlled male voice which alternately placated the driver and joined in his angry cursing. It was the owner of the second voice who hit her gently whenever she began to moan. She was twenty-nine years old and she was not going to be able to hold it much longer. This realization made her feel guilty and she lay a docile lump in the fetal position on the back seat of the Jaguar, jiggling her feet and wondering what on earth was happening.

The second voice seemed not to be speaking to the driver. Was there a telephone in the car?

"The bitch put me on hold."

"Hold?"

"Listen to the goddam music."

A pause and a profane comment from the whiny voiced one. Minutes passed, the noises of traffic and failed attempts to catch a light before it changed continuing; the two voices fallen silent. And then, "We have Mavis Navrone. I will call back in exactly one half-hour."

There was more but now Gloria had at least an inkling of what was going on. She began to squirm and moan and did not stop when the man began beating her with the rolled up newspaper. It proved to be impossible to say that she was not Mavis Navrone, not with a handkerchief stuffed in her mouth. She was so relieved to learn that this was a mistake that she could no longer contain herself.

Dwayne Navrone kept the phone nestled between his left shoulder and ear as Mavis began her third account of the funny phone call she had received.

"It's got to be a joke, Mave."

"Joke?"

"Sure."

"I get a call telling me I have been kidnapped, I know somebody's nuts or trying to be funny. It's like telling me I'm not here."

"Strange."

"Granted it's strange, but it isn't funny. You had to hear his voice."

"Well, anyway he was wrong. Nobody kidnapped you."

"Maybe it's a threat."

He felt like Ray Milland in the movie, calling home from the club expecting to talk to the man he had hired to kill his wife and getting Grace Kelly. From where he sat he could see across the rows of desks to the glass cage in which Jennifer dwelt. She was a high hipped, long legged, large breasted blonde of the kind that had figured in his sexual fantasies since puberty struck shortly before his twelfth birthday. In the twenty years since, he had seen her on billboards, in television commercials, in semi-pornographic films, seductive and pneumatic, a creature whose fate it was to drive men mad. It was for her that he had entered into negotiations with regard to Mavis.

"I don't go out with married men," Jennifer had said the first time they had gone out.

"A man's entitled to one mistake."

"To whom do you refer?"

He slipped his arm around her waist, taking in breath as he did so. No woman had ever seemed so much a woman as did Jennifer and he was still adjusting to the incredible fact that she was receptive to his advances.

Their relationship, as she called it, matured. They went from the office to her apartment on West 12th Street, trying to keep their hands off one another in the cab, bumping and grinding up the narrow stairway to her third floor room, barely making it to the bed in time. The woman was as mad for him as he was for her. It was impossible to think of what he was doing as infidelity or sin. God meant him to go to bed with Jennifer Bailey.

His residual religious sense made it convenient to think that he was simply falling in with the plan of providence when he made love to Jennifer. Oddly, the affair had the effect of increasing his lovemaking with his wife. Not only did Mavis not suspect him of wandering; she felt that their marriage had achieved a new plateau. It reconciled her to keeping her job and putting off yet longer having the babies she dreamed of.

Depleted, sweaty, flat on his back and staring at the ceiling with Jennifer shamelessly nude beside him, the exchange he dreaded would begin.

"I can't go on like this."

"I know."

"What good is that? 'I know'."

"I feel as bad about it as you do."

"Oh? Tell me how bad you feel."

Until desire began again she was just another goddamn woman, wanting what she could not have and unlikely to lay off until she got it. She wanted to marry him. She wanted him to divorce Mavis and marry her and they would spend the rest of their lives in bed, or words to that effect. Geez.

"You got any idea what a divorce is like?"

"You been divorced before?"

"No! Jennifer, I don't have a lot but I have put away a bit." Actually his portfolio was astounding for a man who earned what he did, but then he spent an hour of company time each morning talking with his broker. He studied the market, he read the *Wall Street Journal*; he kept an ear open for tips. But finally he played his gut and he had done very well. If they divorced, Mavis would claim half of what they had and get it. She might quit working and demand support. There were lots of women judges in divorce courts now. Dwayne had heard stories.

"Is that all it is for you, a matter of money?"

Jennifer got out of bed and when she crossed to the bathroom he was again overwhelmed by his colossal luck, getting a woman like that into bed with him. The roll of her buttocks and the reflection of her breasts in the bathroom mirror before she closed the door restored him to the condition that had been his in the taxi ride to her place. How could he ever give up Jennifer and confine his attentions to Mavis alone? What did God want him to do?

He and God decided that he would be a damned fool to take his assets into a divorce court and expect to come out any other way than wishing he had kept his pants zipped. On the other hand, his manifest destiny was Jennifer, not

Mavis. He began to daydream of accidents Mavis might have that would solve his problem. Or at least Jennifer's problem. He himself would have been willing to go on having both of them, but it was clear Jennifer would nag him to death until he got rid of Mavis.

"My psychologist would like to talk to you."

"Your what?"

"The man I go to for counseling."

"You've talked about us?"

"Dwayne, don't be silly. I tell him everything. There'd be no point in going otherwise."

He got onto an elbow and stared at her. It was like hearing she had another man. That became the theme. He had to talk to Dr. Harris.

"A shrink? Not on your life."

"If it weren't for Dr. Harris, I would have stopped this long ago. He helps me reconcile to things."

Harris began to sound like an ally. Eventually Dwayne went and talked to him. It was a real surprise. The solution that emerged was that Mavis had to go. Somehow they had reached an agreement without actually saying it. Harris and an associate named Ruffle could do it. Fifteen apiece, half down, half afterward.

"You sure you can handle this?"

Harris studied his cigarette before looking at Dwayne. "You sure you can handle the thirty."

They never came right out with what it was they were arranging, but they both knew. He brought photographs of Mavis, he described precisely where she worked, on the morning of D-day he phoned Harris and told him what Mavis was wearing and the purse she was carrying.

"It's big as a briefcase, white, you can't miss it."

But Harris and his friend Ruffle had missed it and here

was Mavis on the phone telling him of the call the idiots had put through as per plan to mislead the police. They hadn't kidnapped Mavis. Who the hell had they grabbed?

Mavis dug about in her purse for a tissue but her hand was in a foreign land. And then she understood. Darn Gloria anyway to have bought a purse exactly like hers. The least she could do would be not to carry it to work and save it for weekends. Mavis felt she might be driven to do that herself, and she resented it. She might just as well shop at KMart if everyone else was going to wear and carry exactly the same thing she did. Gloria must have taken the wrong purse to the ladies'.

"Where's Ms. Sheahan?" Jerome Jarbro asked. In his position, he not only used Ms., he tried to pronounce it.

"She'll be right back."

"I've been trying to reach her for twenty minutes."

"Twenty minutes! I'll go see."

As she went down the hall, she noticed the stairway door was open a bit; something caught in it prevented it from closing. She hesitated, then pushed the door, ready to run if God knew what was on the stairway. And then she saw the purse.

She snatched it up, looked defiantly in both directions, but there was no one else in the hallway, then marched to the ladies'. Once inside, she searched the purse. It was hers. So far as she could see nothing was missing. Her billfold was in her desk drawer but there was no sign that the contents of the purse had been rustled. Gloria had just dropped it!

She thought about that. It made no sense and thinking about it gave her a creepy feeling. She hurried back to her office, keeping to the far side of the hall as she went past the stairway door. Jerome Jarbro stood where she had left him, tapping his perforated toe, looking out at the grimy portion of the Manhattan skyline it was their lot to see. From a certain angle, one could sight between the classroom building across the street and its neighbor and see the Chrysler building.

"Mr. Jarbro, something funny is going on."

"You didn't find her."

"I found this." She held up her purse. "It's mine. Mavis must have taken it by mistake. See the one under her desk? They're identical. Anyway, I found mine in the stairway."

It all made sense to her, but Mr. Jarbro was looking at her strangely.

"Let me start at the beginning."

She told him about the weird call informing her that she had been kidnapped. She explained about the identical purses. She put two and two together and added them up for him.

"What I think, Mr. Jarbro, is they meant to kidnap me and mistakenly took Gloria."

"Why would anyone kidnap you?"

She might have taken umbrage at his question, but it was a good one. Any kidnapper expecting to get to Easy Street with any ransom Dwayne could come up with was misinformed. When a kidnapper found out what she was worth he would kill her in disgust. She shivered. But fear for herself gave way to apprehension about Gloria.

"You must call the police," Jerome Jarbro said.

"Me?"

"Who else? You're the only one who can explain what happened."

"But what if she wasn't kidnapped?"

"Do you believe that?"

"That she wasn't?" Mavis thought of the white purse wedged in the doorway to the staircase. She had no doubt that Gloria had been dragged through that doorway and carried down the staircase. "Do you think she was?"

"On the basis of what you tell me, yes."

"I want to speak to my husband."

He lifted her phone from its cradle and handed it to her.

6

Dwayne had a problem.

Mavis had called again and more than ever he felt chained to her in a way that prevented a life of bliss with Jennifer.

"Dwayne, that call? I think they kidnapped Gloria."

"They?"

"Him. Whoever called and said he had me."

Dwayne listened to her babble on and felt as he had when he learned his SAT scores would keep him from going to college, the way he had felt when he opened the letter from Ed McMahon and found that all he'd won was the outdoor gas operated grill. It was very difficult to avoid the thought that he was a loser, condemned to want what was always just out of reach. Jennifer had been within reach; he made his move to make her his and now this.

"You've got identical purses?"

"She took mine, Dwayne."

As near as he could figure, Harris and Ruffle had pulled it off as planned. Everything had gone great with one exception—they had the wrong woman. Given the identical purses, it was hard to see how he could blame them. They had done what they contracted to do. They would demand the rest of the money. Or else. He would be out thirty thousand and still have Mavis while Henny Sheahan would be on the town a free man.

"Should I call the police?"

"To report finding your own purse in the stairwell?"

"Dwayne, Gloria's missing."

"Have you talked to Henny?"

"Henny. They're separated."

It was the way Henny Sheahan had just moved out on Gloria that had set Dwayne's mind to thinking how wonderful life would be if it weren't for Mavis. But Henny had nothing to lose. Not quite true. He lost more by moving out than staying put. Gloria had a steady job, but Henny was always chasing rainbows when he wasn't at the track. The main thing moving out gained him was freedom.

"It's what I want to do I do." His smile was radiant. His Adam's apple rode up and down his throat; he shook a cigarette from his pack and lit it. Gloria had always made him go outside to smoke.

"If you got the wherewithal."

"Hey, I won today."

Fifty bucks and Henny was in clover. Of course he had separated out the hundred he would bet the next day.

"Gloria and I are only good to each other dead."

Insurance on one another was all they had. But Dwayne had his stock accounts and a printout Mavis wouldn't understand even if she was curious about it, which she apparently wasn't. He was damned if he would give up all that. Even for Jennifer. But that added thought was in a different register. What he needed was a way to get rid of Mavis, keep his money and have Jennifer. That was a way he thought he had found when he talked with Calvin Harris.

It had been forty-five minutes since Mavis first called to

tell him of what she thought was a weird and scary phone call. The phone call he had been waiting for had not yet come and his problem was what was he going to tell Harris. Whatever he said would jeopardize Gloria and he sure as hell wasn't going to pay to make Henny a free man. Harris and Ruffle had half the payment and they might settle for that, do Gloria and get the hell out of town, out of the country. Not that they had anything to fear from him.

Call the police and turn in the hitmen who had failed to fulfill a contract? What was the country coming to if a man's word was no longer his bond? The thought he had kept at bay during the past weeks, his mind obscured by sensual images of Jennifer, was that he was making himself vulnerable. If anything went wrong, Harris was sure to finger the man who had put him up to it, all hands going down with the ship, rather than keep quiet, sit for years in jail protecting with his silence a man who had paid only half the agreed upon sum.

The phone rang and his whole body seemed to ring with it. He did not answer until the third ring.

"Yeah."

"Harris. Bingo."

Bingo was code for mission accomplished. Harris had been very heavy on the undercover aspects of the thing, but then he claimed to have been in naval intelligence. "And don't tell me that's an oxymoron." Capped teeth coated with saliva glistened as he smiled.

"What's an oxymoron?"

Ruffle shifted his weight. "Cut the shit."

So they had gone on about procedures. Not answering until the third ring was part of what Harris called the drill.

"Bingo," Dwayne answered and waited.

"Trussed tramp *bene. Più tarde.*"

Harris hung up. The bound Gloria had been taken to Hoboken without incident. Harris would call later. In his wallet Dwayne had a slip of paper with the number of a public phone in Morristown. In maybe half an hour his phone would ring again, he would answer and the connection would be broken on the other end. Then he was to call the number on the slip from a public phone as soon as possible. Harris would be waiting and they could then talk on "clear channel." The first ridiculous exchange made it clear that Harris did not yet know he had made a mistake.

7

Except for hitting every blessed red light cross-town Ruffle was feeling pretty good. Cussing out the lights underlined how well everything else had gone, and he was waiting for Harris to give him the old thumbs up. He had positioned himself by the slightly opened stairway door, relying on the report Harris had painstakingly put together. At 1:40 p.m., subject to restroom.

"Every day?"

"Like clock work. The human bladder is a marvelous creation."

Ruffle nodded, hoping to escape a lecture on the marvels of the human bladder. What he got was a lecture on the human being as creature of habit. "To some degree a function of biology, granted. At any rate, she micturates every afternoon within an hour after returning from lunch."

"Micturates?"

"Takes a piss."

"You said 1:40."

"Just an average. The trouble is there's a traffic jam of women at that time."

That's why the purse was important. That's why it was necessary to come into the hallway after spotting the purse to make sure there weren't a lot of other women about.

"What if there are?"

"We try when she goes back."

"What if there are others around then?"

"We come back another day."

After all the dry runs Ruffle groaned at the prospect. Harris was a perfectionist. He really loved working out a schedule, thinking everything out beforehand, going through it again and again until it was automatic.

"This way we make no mistakes."

And the thing had gone off like clockwork. Ruffle spotted the purse, stepped into an empty hallway, slipped the plastic bag over the woman's shoulders and dragged her through the door Harris held open and then they were hustling her down the stairs like a bag of laundry. She fought like a tiger when he reached inside with the handkerchief from her bag and stuffed it into her mouth while Harris was tying her hands. If anything was going to go wrong it would have been then. They were working on her just inside the steel door leading into the parking lot where the car waited. If anyone came in, Code Red would have gone into effect.

"Code Red?"

"No witnesses."

It brought home the point of grabbing the woman. Her husband was anxious for her to receive her eternal reward, as Harris insisted on putting it, and they were to act as the angels of mercy.

"What's that smell?"

They were waiting at what could be the last red light before the tunnel and the car was suddenly full of sharp sickening odor.

"The subject has been incontinent."

"In the back seat!"

There was a miserable groan from the plastic sack.

"We interrupted her schedule," Harris said, unperturbed, but he cracked his window a little.

Telephoning Mavis's office to let them know they had taken the woman hadn't gone so well, and Harris was very angry when he had been put on hold. But the message had been sent, and that was the main thing.

When they emerged from the tunnel, Harris picked up the phone again, letting the client know they had succeeded and were in Jersey with his wife.

For the next call, Harris had to leave the car to use the public phone in front of a deli. He handed Ruffle a rolled up copy of *Country Gentleman*. "Keep her quiet." There was a muffled sound from the plastic bag and he gave her a whack.

The subject was silent during Harris's absence but Ruffle gave her a couple whacks anyway. After less than two minutes, Harris came running back to the car, madder than hell. Ruffle got ready to roll and had them moving while Harris was still shutting the door. He reached over the seat and there was the sound of plastic tearing and then the terrified face of the woman showed up in the rearview mirror, an ear of the handkerchief emerging from the corner of her mouth. Harris grabbed it and pulled it out.

"What's your name?"

Her answer was a banshee wail, a scream that lifted the hairs on the back of Ruffle's head. Harris took a swing at her and she went out of sight, ducking the blow. He was kneeling in the passenger seat now, the better to get at her. He got her sitting up again.

"Who the hell are you?"

The woman was hysterical. Well, she had been through an experience. Ruffle was beginning to get uneasy at the

34

question Harris was asking. It took him three minutes to get an answer.

"Gloria," the woman sobbed. "Gloria Sheahan."

"Jesus," Harris said.

That's when Ruffle knew that despite all the planning and practicing and the clockwork efficiency they had made a very big mistake indeed.

8

Jerome Jarbro's mother had not raised him to be head of the department of student financial aid at Lyndon Johnson Community College or of any other institution remotely like it. He was meant to be a college professor like her father who had taught English in a very fine private liberal arts college in the state of Missouri and was in every way a wise and cultivated and gentle man. Jerome had never met this legendary maternal grandfather. He had died before Ellen Glasgow Hines Jarbro could afford the trip to Missouri with her son.

"Ellen Glasgow was a particular favorite of his."

And consequently of his mother's. She read all the books by the novelist, as did Jerome himself when he grew older. Jerome's father had made little impression on his mother's memory. He had been in the Air Force when they met and the fact that he had a family in the East doubtless conjured up Ellen Glasgow settings. The reality was in harsh contrast to these romantic expectations. The Jarbros lived in Queens, the father a bookkeeper who went the rounds of his clients to work in their offices or worked out of the apartment in Queens. Major Jarbro and his bride found a place in the Village, another of Ellen's dreams, and Jerome was born while his father was in Vietnam. Major Jarbro was shot down and to this day Jerome had no idea whether he was dead or alive. His mother had reluctantly allied herself with the wives of other MIAs. She refused the invitation to move in with her in-laws in Queens, waited in vain for the suggestion that she return with her son to Missouri and meanwhile supported herself as a copy editor because she could work on manuscripts at home. She also prepared indexes for books.

"I don't really consider it work," she always said. "Nothing to do with books is work."

"Says you," said old Jarbro, but he meant books of another kind.

Ellen's stepmother got Professor Jarbro's pension when he died suddenly in his fifties. Jerome was raised to take the legendary father's place.

"He took his doctorate from Columbia. So will you."

The money was no problem, thanks to Grandpa Jarbro who, it turned out, had done very well. The problem was that Jerome had no particular bent for English. It wasn't just the novels of Ellen Glasgow; he found that he disliked all fiction. Poetry seemed to him an abuse of language. He was good at math and took to computers. His mother was appalled at the emerging prospect that Jerome would take after his paternal not his maternal grandfather. But so it was to be. It was an old friend of Grandpa Jarbro's who got Jerome in at LJCC.

"He cheated in school," the old man said with an indulgent smile. "He should be in prison."

But the old friend had gone into politics and he managed to push Jerome's application through. Only later did Jerome learn that his grandfather had paid two thousand dollars for the favor. Jerome still lived with his mother in the apartment in which she had raised him. Her eyes had weakened to such an extent that she no longer edited. She spent summers on a park bench doling out crumbs to pigeons. She also liked McDonald's where cups and forks and everything were thrown out after use.

"I don't want to catch AIDS."

"From a hamburger?"

But she studied him closely. Any time he had shown interest in a girl, she had interfered and now that he was a bachelor in his thirties she was fearful he would become a homosexual and bring home the dreaded disease. It was Jerome's fate to fall in love with a married woman, Mavis Navrone, whom he could only worship from afar. The disappearance of Gloria Sheahan was the kind of opportunity he had prayed for.

"They have made a mistake," he said to Mavis. "You're right. Why else that phone call?"

She put her hand on his sleeve, overcome with the horror of it. He lay his hand atop hers, it was a natural thing to do, he was her superior and he was comforting her during this moment of terror.

"You should come to my office and try to relax."

"Relax!"

"There, there." How soft her skin was, softer than he had imagined when he studied her through the blinds that shielded his office window from his underlings. Weekends he sometimes took the train to New Rochelle and walked past where she lived, not knowing what he would say if he should run into her there, but excited by the prospect. He had caught glimpses of her with her husband, a man he hated instantly and on principle. He was one of the tall, swaggering kind Jerome felt intimidated by. It was unpleasant to think of his own meager attractions compared with those of such an Adonis. But it was clear to Jerome that Mavis had what brains there were in the family. The reports he made on her performance twice a year were hymns of praise. He had worshipped her for three years but today was the first day he had actually touched her. He felt almost dizzy when she did not remove her hand from his arm. He led her to his office and she came along docilely.

He installed her across the desk and filled her a cup from his personal Mr. Coffee.

"Call Henny."

"Henny?"

"Gloria's husband. They're separated but he should know."

She sat erectly in the chair, her knees turned to one side, the short skirt stopping inches above her knees. Her hair, her eyes, her mouth—everything about her was more perfect than he had thought. Because of what he knew, he felt less guilty about his feelings for her. Gloria Sheahan was separated. Perhaps Mavis would be too. Did she suspect what he had learned about her husband?

Learned quite by accident. When he saw the couple coming toward him he had thought only that the man was the same type as Mavis's husband, and then he realized it was Dwayne Navrone. The woman with him was a caricature, parted lips, clinging to him, her ripe body seeming about to burst from her dress.

Jerome let them pass, turned and followed them. He followed them into a Chinese restaurant and took the booth next to theirs, out of sight but not out of hearing. There was no mistaking their conversation. They were lovers, recovering from a bout in her apartment, gathering strength to return. Jerome had the shrimp fried rice and dallied until they were done and then again followed them to the building on West 12th. The lobby door was locked and the mailboxes were inside but within days he had her name. Jennifer Bailey. She worked in the same office as Dwayne.

Jerome had gathered all this information because, although it meant sadness for Mavis it represented opportunity for himself. Now here they sat in his office as the result of the disappearance of Gloria Sheahan. The circumstances had cast him in a favorable light, someone to lean on, someone in control.

"Do you know the number of Gloria's husband?"

The question seemed to surprise her. She stared at him.

"No. I don't know. He moved out but where?"

She made an impatient noise but Jerome wished they could sit like this forever.

9

Whatever else Henny did, he never hit her. Gloria hadn't been treated like this since she was a kid and made the mistake of fighting with her brother. She was in a nightmare and the wonder was she hadn't lost her mind. A sack pulled over her head, then that awful hand groping over her and stuffing a handkerchief into her mouth while her hands were tied behind her back. And then to lose control and wet her pants!

But none of that had been as horrible as being slapped and beaten after the sack had been removed. Who were these maniacs?

"What's your name?"

He took a swing at her and she ducked. She realized she was screaming. She had been screaming ever since he pulled the handkerchief from her mouth.

"Who are you?"

She told him finally. They thought she was Mavis! Dear God, this was all a mistake. They had done all this by mistake, they thought she was someone else.

"Why did you think I was Mavis Navrone?" At the moment she would volunteer to help them kidnap Mavis if they'd let her go.

But he had turned around and ignored her question.

The driver started to say something and was told to shut up.

"I have to think."

"You and your thinking."

His hand went toward the driver, but he stopped it, and put his hand on the other's shoulder.

"Let's just go ahead with it."

The driver hesitated, nodded, and then the speed of the car increased. Gloria was thrown backward. Weren't they going to let her go? They had thought she was Mavis, what was the point?

"Untie my hands."

They ignored her. She sat in the middle of the back seat until she saw her tear streaked face and the mess of her hair in the rearview mirror. She slid over behind the driver and looked out the side window and for the first time noticed the scenery flying by, not just the other cars but beyond, open fields, things growing, woods. Where were they? Nothing looked familiar at all. But a highway sign informed her they were in New Jersey and that Morristown was only seven miles away. She could not have been more surprised if they were nearing Beirut or Baghdad.

The man in the passenger seat turned to look at her. He wore a fastidious expression as if she didn't measure up to his expectations. Well, she didn't think a lot of him either, or of the man behind the wheel for that matter.

"Where are you taking me?"

"Lie down."

All she could think to do was stick out her tongue at him but when he swung his fist, she dropped onto her side. It made her furious to be treated this way, but there just didn't seem to be anything she could do about it. The fact that they hadn't even meant to kidnap her added to her sense of being badly treated. Why on earth wasn't all this happening to Mavis?

Mavis. The word formed in her mind and there was a reason but she couldn't think of it, couldn't bring it in front of her mind. Why would they mistake her for Mavis rather than any other woman working in the office of financial aid? Or man. No, they wouldn't have made that dumb a mistake.

Gloria closed her eyes and reconstructed in her mind getting up from her desk, taking her purse and heading for the ladies'. The purse! She and Mavis had identical purses. Someone might have seen the purse, thought she was Mavis . . .

She said aloud, "Mavis Navrone."

Silence from the front seat and then the fastidious one was looking down at her.

"What did you say?"

"I know why you thought I was Mavis Navrone."

"Why?"

"My purse. We have identical purses."

His expression was all she needed. She was right. She closed her eyes, shutting him out, but then her head rang with the power of his hand striking her and her eyes popped open.

"Stop hitting me!" she screamed.

"Hit you? Lady, we're going to kill you."

Anger gave way to terror and she lay sobbing, turning her face toward the back of the seat, her right arm numb from the pressure of her body lying on it. It was so terrible, this happening to her, she had never harmed anyone, never even wished harm to Henny although God knows he deserved it. Finally he had left her and she wasn't even surprised. They called it a separation but what it meant was that he could no longer freeload off her, steal her money and throw it away at the track. Mavis kidded her about going out with other guys, but where does a thirty-two year old woman go to meet guys she would want to be seen with let alone anything more? Of course it was the anything more Mavis meant.

As a girl Gloria had lived in dread that she would have a vocation and have to join the convent and live like a china doll the rest of her life, but the big thing was that then she couldn't get married and have a family and know all the enjoyments of life. What a laugh that was. She had married Henny and there were no kids and as for enjoyment, marriage was a lot like putting your finger in a pencil sharpener. Now she thought of what a cushy deal nuns had, at least in those days, no worries, all prim and starched and organized, each hour accounted for, doing good. In the back seat of the Jaguar with her hands tied behind her and her arm numb she sobbed with regret that she had not entered the convent when she had the chance.

She turned her head and watched the trees go by, close, they must be on another road. A few minutes later, the car slowed, turned and bumped to a stop. When the engine was turned off there was a moment of complete silence and then the squeak of the doors being opened. She continued to lie still, with her legs pressed tightly together and her wet underclothes uncomfortable on her flesh, stinging, embarrassing. The back door opened, her ankle was grabbed and she was pulled ignominiously out of the car. She used her shoulder to protect herself, and her elbow to the degree she could as she tumbled out onto the ground. They were treating her like garbage because they intended to put her out with the trash. That realization got her to her knees and then she was on her feet. The two men were going toward a cabin-like house surrounded by woods. Gloria began to run toward the trees, hobbling along as if her feet were tied, not her hands. Her breath was painful in her chest and she wobbled as she walked, unable to balance herself with her arms.

"Hey!"

The angry voice spurred her on and she tried to run faster. They were coming after her, she could hear the sound of footsteps and then just as she got to the woods, there was a terrible pain in her side as the tackler's head banged into her and then she was tumbling to the ground with the little monkey who had driven the car all over her. Unbelievably he forced her onto her back and began to squirm on top of her, as fully dressed as she was. And she began to laugh.

It was the silliest performance she had ever heard of and once she started to laugh she went hysterically on. The man stopped squirming and looked down at her with a devastated expression on his face that made her laugh even harder. Then the weight was gone. His partner had pulled him off her and sent him sprawling along the ground. He reached down, rolled her onto her side, took her elbow and helped her to her feet. He kept his hand under her elbow when she was standing and directed her toward the cabin. As they moved along, from time to time a giggle escaped her. Her escort was laughing too.

Couldn't they all be friends? Couldn't they just laugh and admit the whole thing was foolish and call it off?

He said, "In France there's a monastery of the Laughing Jesus."

"What an awful thing to say!"

"It's true."

He helped her up the steps and across the porch of the cabin and pulled open the screen door. He bowed and she went inside to the smell of stale wood smoke and pent-up air. The one thing she wanted to see, a telephone, was not in sight. A couch facing the fireplace was covered with a fabric of colorful design. There was an oval woven rug on which sat a low large table with ancient magazines and a vase full of pussy willows. The walls were of shellacked plywood. So was the door to which her captor walked her and then opened. Stairs led upward. He nodded at Gloria.

"Your quarters, Madame."

There was the sound of heavy footsteps on the porch and the little man burst into the room carrying a gun so large it took two hands to hold it. He trained it on his companion.

"All right, you sonofabitch. Laugh."

The other man laughed. He threw back his head and let out a great roar. Gloria watched in horror, expecting this to ignite the little man to something horrible. But the gun drooped and a sheepish expression came over his face. He walked toward his companion, the gun held by one hand at his side. Tears seemed to be running down the other's face. He threw his arm over the little man's shoulders and for a moment they stood there laughing. Suddenly, the larger man spun the other one around, snatched the gun from him and pushed him toward the door. He lifted a leg and put a shoe between the other's shoulder blades and gave a great push that sent the little man reeling toward the door. The momentum carried him right on through because the screen door splintered under his weight. The larger man stepped over the debris and a moment later there was a terrible burst of sound.

Gloria ran up the stairs into the suffocating heat of an attic.

10

Henny Sheahan was well within the speed limit when he was pulled over on his way back from the track. He always drove slowly after a run of bad luck. When the flashing gumball showed up in his mirror, he had been figuring how much he could get for a car that he still owed as much on as he did this one. He pulled onto the berm, stopped and rolled onto his left haunch to dig out his billfold. He had his license ready when the trooper showed up at his window.

"You Henny Sheahan?" The voice was not the voice of an arresting officer. Henny detected something like sympathy in the fat Irish face.

"Yeah." He displayed his license as verification but the cop ignored it.

"Something's happened to your wife."

The simple declarative sentence started a riot of thoughts in Henny's mind. Of course, he assumed the trooper meant Gloria was dead and he would have had to be a better man than he was if he hadn't realized that he was now worth three hundred thousand before taxes. He managed to keep a straight face.

"What do you mean, something's happened?"

"I don't know much. The Manhattan police want to talk to you."

"Damn it, what's happened to my wife?"

His lower lip actually trembled, as if he were about to cry. Maybe he was. He had loved Gloria enough to marry her, and even though things hadn't turned out the way either of them hoped, she was still his wife. Their separation was just a deal between themselves, nothing legal. He had actually used the fact of the insurance policy on his life as a reason for doing it that way. At least dead he could do her some good.

She had bawled at that, of course, and for a while there it looked like he wasn't going to get out from under her thumb after all. She took him in her arms and crushed those great boobs against him and if there hadn't been an NBA playoff he had to get some money down on who knows? She was taking all the blame for everything when he went out the door.

"This is better for you," he called over his shoulder. Five hundred on the Blazers and he could be rolling in it.

The trooper shifted his weight to the creak of leather and jangle of metal. "She's been kidnapped."

"Kidnapped! What the hell for?"

Apparently you were given a quota of stupid things to say in such circumstances. The cop just shrugged, gave him the address of the precinct and saluted. Henny saluted back and he might have been a recruit at San Diego getting in good with the drill instructor. The trooper actually stopped a lane of traffic so Henny could get back onto the highway.

He got his thoughts in a line. One, they had figured he was at the track which is why the trooper had picked him up at this time on this highway. Two, Gloria kidnapped? It made no sense. People kidnapped for money, for ransom, and who the hell could pay anything to get Gloria back. Her husband? The best he could do would be to make the kidnappers beneficiaries of his insurance. Three, insurance. It was just cold realism to recognize that few if any kidnap victims are ever released unharmed. Kidnappers couldn't run the risk of being identified by their victim. His first thought had been of that $300,000 and if he didn't get it now he was going to feel cheated. It would be like losing every race for the rest of his life. Of course he would quit gambling once he had the money. Why run the risk when you already had what you ran the risk for? On the other hand, imagine setting aside a fraction, say, fifty thou, and betting that judiciously. Double it, say. Stash half, and start over again. Hell, he could run the stake up to a million without risking his principal.

Coming over the bridge the thought struck him that Gloria had been kidnapped to put pressure on where she worked, Lyndon Johnson Community College. Would LJCC pop to get Gloria back alive? He tried not to resent the thought. It was as if someone was horning in on something personal. But it got worse. Gloria was always full of stories of the threats she got from students wanting financial aid. Some had neglected to enroll but figured it was just another form of welfare and all they had to do was apply.

"Not that it's much more difficult," Gloria added. "But they've got to be full time students. I don't make the rules."

He could see her sitting at her desk saying that to some linebacker type who wanted the financial aid in cash.

"They think we write them out a check!" Gloria shook her head. Her estimate of college kids had plummeted since she went to work at LJCC. "When I tell them that what it means is they don't have to pay anything for the classes, no tuition, they act as if it's some kind of a con."

She had years worth of disgruntled applicants. Henny

imagined some guy, he was always the size of an NBA center, brooding over Gloria's decision and then deciding to act.

The only way he could drive such depressing thoughts away was to remind himself that he didn't know what the hell had happened. Maybe some horny kid in the neighborhood had kidnapped her to turn her into a sex slave. Stranger things had happened.

At the precinct he pulled into an empty space reserved for official vehicles only and hurried inside. He stopped at the first desk.

"My name's Henny Sheahan."

It was a woman of sorts behind the desk. She wore a suit and a dress shirt open at the neck and huge earrings lest the short haircut utterly confuse you. She was waiting.

"Gloria Sheahan's husband. The one who got kidnapped?"

"How many's she got?"

A comedian. Had he expected a welcoming committee when he came through the door? Maybe he should have confessed to a crime. He felt that he had committed one when the lady cop of sorts conferred with her colleagues who knew as little as she did. It was when he mentioned LJCC that they got the picture.

"Cable," they said. "That's his."

"Where is he?"

A search for Cable was launched. Henny hoped all these jokers were on the take because they sure as hell weren't doing the taxpayer any good. But then Cable came in, explaining that he had been in the men's room.

"I shoulda looked," Henny said, hoping to get a laugh out of the lady cop of sorts, but she just let her mouth droop and tipped her head.

"James Branch Cable. How did you hear about your wife?"

"A trooper stopped me."

They were weaving among the desks to a glass enclosed office. Inside a fan stirred the loose papers on the desk, the smell of cigarette smoke was heavy, and the noise from outside was still audible.

"Your tax dollars at work."

"We live in New Rochelle."

"We?"

"Gloria and I."

"I heard you moved out."

"What the hell has happened to her?"

Cable tipped back in his chair then grabbed the desk when it threatened to topple over. He moved it and got the back wedged against the wall. He lit the cigarette he had been in the process of taking out.

"You smoke?"

"Only second-hand smoke."

"You got something against smoking?"

"Do I look like the Surgeon General?"

Cable narrowed his eyes as if he were seeking a resemblance. Wow. Henny decided to play these guys straight as an arrow.

"Grow yourself an Amish beard and maybe."

He let it go and then Cable told him what had happened to Gloria. The details made him feel like a shit for thinking first of the insurance money. The poor girl. Cable had put Gloria's white purse on the desk. He reached for it, but Cable pulled it back. Henny wondered if the detective knew he wanted to see how much money Gloria had been hauling around.

"That your wife's purse?"

"You know it is."

Cable had the saddest face Henny had seen since the end of the eighth race. The suit looked like it was off the rack at Wal-Mart. He smoked generic brand cigarettes.

"This purse belongs to Mavis Navrone."

"Naw. It's Gloria's."

Cable explained. Mavis and Gloria had bought identical purses and Gloria had taken Mavis's by mistake.

"We think the kidnappers took your wife by mistake."

"Mistake!"

"They called in to say they had Mavis Navrone."

"What a kick in the ass."

Cable nodded, so apparently he didn't realize Henny was referring to the disappearance of all his hopes.

"How much they asking?"

"They haven't asked for anything yet."

"You talked to Dwayne?"

"You know Mr. Navrone?"

Henny shrugged. "More or less. The girls had a get-together a couple times. You know."

"You get along?"

"Why not? You saw Mavis, didn't you?"

"What do you mean?"

"Anyone who can't get along with a bod like that is crazy."

"You find her attractive?"

"Don't you?"

"I'm on duty."

11

Blasting after the fleeing Ruffle with the machine pistol he had wrested from his partner gave Calvin Harris an odd sense of satisfaction. He would have said that he was impatient of imperfection, but the fact of the matter was that to call his life and his deeds imperfect was to sin on the side of understatement.

It is no bed of roses to be born the son of a minister of the gospel, to come to consciousness seated in a front pew with one's father fulminating from the pulpit above and one's mother stiffly endorsing every jot and tittle of the paternal sermon. In adolescence he had tried to imagine his parents as insincere, however unconsciously. Having lost his own faith, inherited at best, he found it impossible to believe that someone as intelligent as his father actually believed the basic tenets of Christian revelation.

"Jesus is the central event of human history?" Even to say it seemed to Calvin a negative comment on it.

The jowls his father had developed, great flabby dewlaps that created the effect of a St. Bernard, added to the authority of his manner. "The alpha and the omega, Calvin."

Pastor Harris believed that the deceased members of an unevolved human race in all their billions would eventually be restored to life, the dust collected and life breathed into it again, and then a great judgment would take place, the separation of the sheep from the goats. Calvin was not in doubt as to what it was his parents believed; he knew it as well as they did by the time he realized that he could no longer subscribe to such things as true. A carnal itch had taken him down paths he preferred not to remember later, but it became necessary for him to think that his sordid adventures did not matter. They were fleeting episodes, a few minutes out of the expanse of his life. Why should he be defined by those minutes rather than the hours and weeks and months and years?

"We are always sinning, Calvin."

The name he bore was more than a linguistic reminder of his christening. It suggested the sternest and most unbending interpretation of the gospel. Thoughts of dropping it, of using a nickname came and went; he kept it as a sign of contradiction. In the seminary he led his class, but he might have been gathering evidence for his great rebellion. His practice sermons were followed with fascination and with growing unease on the part of the faculty, but they could not really think that the son of the Reverend Doctor Franklin Harris could possibly preach heterodoxy. Shortly before he would have been called, he staged the Great Apostasy, informing a chock full campus church that he no longer believed a single article of the Nicene Creed. There were those who had exempted the statement of Christ's birth from their doubt, but Calvin Harris was ready to believe that no Christian would recognize as Christ the child that had been born in Bethlehem. Restless murmuring, then the banging of hymnals on the pews, finally a rising to the feet to condemn the preacher. He left the pulpit and strode across the sanctuary shedding his gown and before disappearing from view, stopped and ceremoniously shook the dust of the place from his shoes.

His previous life had led up to that great moment. His life since had descended from it. During the past seven years, when he had delivered himself into the hands of the devil in whom he disbelieved, he had not enjoyed the fruits of his rebellion. Defecting clerics were a drug on the market. There was no way in which he could capitalize on his rejection of Christianity. He wasn't news. The deed by which he had created a great chasm between himself and the whole past of family and indeed of the Christian West, meant little beyond the shocked circle of his former fellow seminarians.

He had given up God for the world, but the world proved to be anything but appreciative, let alone remunerative. He should have read *Faust* more carefully. One who sups with the devil should use a long spoon. His income as a counselor was good but did not make him a wealthy man. It grated on him that he should have lost the great dream of heaven only to be shut out of the earthly kingdom too.

It was while watching television coverage of a protest at an abortion clinic that the seeds of his new vocation were sown. Given their beliefs, the protestors were of course right. The slaughter of the innocent should be protested with every ounce of one's being. It was their opponents who were confused. They spoke as if they were defending great principles, rather than the fundamental principle that the only principles that can govern my choices are those I choose. It was this genial nihilism that Calvin Harris decided consistently to choose.

He would become an instrument of death because he chose to do so.

But for a fee. He did not propose to be a benevolent agent, doing gratis the deed that others did not dare to do themselves. They would pay dearly for his services, far more dearly than they imagined. Of course he wanted their money. But even more he wanted their souls. He opened an office as an astral counselor, he ran an ad in the yellow pages, his services were offered in the personals of the *New York Review of Books*, *National Review* and the *Village Voice*. He prospered. Send me your tired, your rich, your yearning masses and I will lighten the burden of their wealth and counsel them along the path of what was once called perdition. It was through the lovely Jennifer that he had been brought indirectly into contact with Dwayne Navrone.

"I'm in love with a married man."

Her opening line, spoken half defiantly, half ashamedly. It had reminded Ambrose Ruffle of hearing confessions. Coming to know Ruffle the runaway priest had not a little to do with the character of Calvin's professional practice. Jennifer Bailey's eyes had roamed the walls before she spoke, she had seen his doctorate from the University of Chicago.

"What's divinity?"

"A white, very sweet sugar candy that melts in your mouth and does not satisfy your hunger."

Her wide pink mouth opened until a film of saliva burst like a bubble. She liked him. People did. Particularly women? Perhaps. Seminary studies train one to appeal to the feminine in the soul. She had not expected wit and humor. Of course it was calculated. No one who could respond to a joke is in a state of despair. Only those who had lost all hope could expect to avail themselves of his services.

"You did not choose to enter life, but the leaving of it is in your hands."

His imagination could not encompass the fascination felt for suicide on the part of the despondent. How can nothingness appeal when going on may be so full of surprises? But then he was not yet forty. Who knew what he would feel when age and all the ills that flesh is heir to began to take their toll? But it was not his own desires he catered to but those of his clients. If they wanted out, if they saw death as simply an ending, not a prelude to anything else, then he would assist them. Most chose to administer a swift and painless drug. He had never been implicated in the deed. The payments he received were clearly for consultations in his office and these were covered by professional confidentiality.

"The seal of the confessional," Ruffle murmured. He had the unfortunate habit of sneering at his past beliefs, a protective attitude, suggesting they still had a hold on him. Ruffle had married and divorced since leaving the priesthood. His office was down the hall from Harris's. The influx of disenchanted clergy into psychological counseling is a remarkable phenomenon, though hardly surprising. Once you have learned to meddle with other people's souls, it is difficult to stop. No wonder that Ruffle, listening to the tape of Jennifer's first visit and her opening words, "I'm in love with a married man," had been reminded of hot stuffy hours in the confessional.

She wanted to talk about it with a stranger who would not pass adverse judgment on what she was doing. How tediously dull the passions of others seem, particularly when they are narrated in a suite of clichés. Jennifer's beautiful head was stuffed with the philosophy of life available on television and in paperback romances of the most incendiary sort. She was sexually active, in the phrase, but her view of the activity was pre-pubescent. A self-contained event that was supposed to absorb her completely into itself, an eternal moment. Only the repetition of the act could make up for its disappointing evanescence even when artfully prolonged. Jennifer was an acrobat of the mattress who wished to see herself as a tragic figure because she could not marry the man with whom once a week for several hours she ran through her repertoire of misbehavior.

Of course she saw what she was doing as wrong. It was meant to be, she couldn't help doing it, but it was wrong. Hers was a Calvinism of the flesh, a carnal predestination.

"You wish to marry him?"

"He's already married."

"If he were free?"

"Of course!"

Calvin doubted that her partner in sin felt the same, but it turned out that he did. Jennifer at first resisted the suggestion that her lover come for a session with Dr. Harris.

"Gratis, of course."

"I've told him I've been coming to you."

"He was flattered?"

"Flattered?"

"Jennifer, he has become the center of your life."

Dwayne Navrone was handsome in a Mediterranean sort of way, awkward when he entered the office. He looked around.

"Where's the couch?"

"That chair is Lazy Boy."

This seemed to reassure him. He sat and pushed the lever and found himself suddenly supine.

"How do I straighten this out?"

"Why don't we just leave it like that for now?"

That was the fateful beginning of a process which now found Calvin Harris on the porch of a cottage near Morristown, New Jersey, firing at his partner in crime, the bullets kicking up dust all around the fleeing former priest. Harris eased up on the trigger, lest he hit the car.

12

Jerome Jarbro in a stressful situation was a wonder and Mavis found herself filled with gratitude as she sat in his office trying to get some perspective on the confusing and frightening events of the afternoon. She had talked with Detective Cable right here in Mr. Jarbro's office with Jerome present and after Cable left she sat on, having her fourth cup from his Mr. Coffee. He should put in at least another half spoonful when be brewed it, but she was not about to say anything critical of him. It was painful to remember the way she and Gloria had joked about the man, hooting over his directives and what had seemed his schoolmarmish insistence on following the rules. At the moment, his rectitude gave Mavis something reassuring to lean upon.

"I don't know what I would have done if it had been you rather than Mrs. Sheahan."

The office outside was empty, the desks closed and covered and abandoned for the day, the setting sun sent slanted bars through the blinds. He had spoken softly, unsurely, but the intent of his words was clear. She could ignore them, pretend she hadn't caught his meaning, or—or what? She looked up into his sheepish eyes. He reminded her of a kid she had gone out with in high school who hadn't known anything about anything. Finally she had placed one of his hands on her hip, slid her arm about him and lifted her lips to his. Within minutes she was fighting him off. Jerome Jarbro looked like that, eager, innocent, not knowing what to do next. She put out her hand and he took it.

"I don't know how I could have gotten through this without you, Jerome."

She had never called him Jerome before, but then she had never held hands with him before. It seemed a major act of infidelity holding hands with someone like Jerome. It dawned on her that it was hours since she'd talked to Dwayne and he hadn't offered to come console her. He showed more sympathy for Henny than he did for her. He didn't seem to realize, as Jerome did, that she had been the intended kidnap victim, and that Gloria had been taken by mistake.

"The question is," Jerome said, "when will they try again?"

"Again!"

He smiled grimly. "Mavis, they came for you and took Gloria. They will want to correct their mistake."

"My God, I never thought of that."

"You can't go home to New Rochelle."

She was surprised he knew where she lived. It was clear he had given the matter some thought. His suggestion was that she use his apartment; he could stay with a friend, and she would be safe.

"Jerome, I can't put you out of your place."

"I'm offering it, you're not putting me out."

"Do you live alone?"

"My mother lives with me."

His mother? She and Gloria had giggled about his probable sexual orientation but the past few hours had con-

vinced Mavis that Jerome Jarbro was all man, what there
was of him.

"I'll have to tell my husband."

He shook his head, looking intently at her. "No, you
mustn't do that."

"I can't just not come home without telling him where I
am."

The thing took on the aspects of an adventure. Jerome
was right that the kidnappers would try again since they had
made a mistake the first time. But she still found it hard to
believe that they would have tried once. Frightened as she
was, Mavis could not see the point in anyone's kidnapping
her. God knows there was no money to be had. Even with
the two of them working, their place in New Rochelle was
modest. They scraped together money for extras, a vacation
to the Bahamas, a trip to Las Vegas. What did they have in
the bank besides the government savings bonds she had
taken out of her check? One hundred dollars face value
once a month, twelve hundred dollars a year, if she lived
long enough it might seem worth it. And her pension. The
great attraction of working at LJCC was the pension. It was
far better than Dwayne's. She looked at Jerome.

"What happens to my retirement if I should die?"

"There's a death benefit."

She stood. "I'm going to the washroom."

Just saying it brought it all back. She looked at Jerome,
he looked at her, and somehow she was in his arms. Going
to the washroom had become a risky thing.

"I'll walk you there."

And he did. It was like a date. They might have been
holding hands, walking so closely side by side. Had Jerome
thought of the pension death benefit before? Was that why
he had made the strange remark that she shouldn't tell

Dwayne where she was spending the night? She moved toward the wall when they passed the stairway door and Jerome moved with her. At the washroom, she hesitated before going in, as if she should say goodbye. A moment later, leaning over a basin, looking at herself in the mirror, she smiled at Jerome's solicitous attitude. Still, it was nice to be fussed over. The police had questioned her and gone. Dwayne hadn't even offered to come take her home. Only Jerome seemed to realize what a traumatic experience this was.

And then the thought came and she watched it form in her eyes. She had been a fool not to notice before how Jerome felt about her. Maybe Gloria had and that's why she'd made fun of him. Now Jerome wanted her to take his apartment for the night, staying with his aged mother, and not tell anyone where she was, not the police, not Dwayne. Only Jerome would know. It was like kidnapping her.

Was Jerome Jarbro behind what had happened to Gloria and should have happened to her? Did he want to make up for a botched job by getting her to his apartment without anyone noticing? His motive was clear. He wanted to ravish her. She breathed on the mirror and wrote "HELP" with her little finger.

Of course she didn't believe a word of this. She decided to accept Jerome's offer to spend the night with his mother in his apartment in the Village. And she would be far more responsive to the poor devil from now on. God knows Dwayne had become more perfunctory in the love department, as if he were doing her a favor, and a girl likes attention.

13

Jennifer Bailey had wasted a year of her life in modeling school, hoping the trend would change, but when she had graduated they still wanted only girls who looked as if they were suffering from anorexia.

"You would have been a favorite courtesan in the Renaissance." Enid the Headmistress laid her large long-nailed hand firmly on Jennifer's thigh. "Men are into meatless women, so to speak."

But it was women who controlled the fashion industry, women—and men who wished they were. Why didn't they like models with a body? Jennifer tried a crash diet and lost ten pounds and then grossed out, eating nonstop for three days until she had gained them all back and more.

"I could give you a position here," Enid said.

"Doing what?"

"We could call it special assistant."

Later Jennifer marveled that she had had the courage to say no to that. At the time, any connection with modeling seemed preferable to the great drab world outside. But she had walked away and on the strength of a high school computer course got the job where she met Dwayne. Great as he was in bed, it seemed like modeling school all over again, a lot of effort with no future. She could stand not being married to him if only she was the only woman in his life. She knew girls who made a big thing about living the way men did, doing it with anyone you wanted, no long term attachments, but Jennifer had no desire to be a serial killer. Still, when she finally took the same friend's advice and went to talk with Dr. Harris, she made the fact that Dwayne was a married man seem like the main problem.

Harris was a surprise.

All he talked about the first session was religion even when she told him she didn't have any. What were her views on the immortality of the soul?

"Do you mean coming back again in another body?"

"Say I did mean that."

"That's nuts."

It was pretty clear he preferred negative answers, so that's what she gave him. The second session he told her that what they were going to do together was construct her personal philosophy of life, her religion.

"That's the best offer I've had all day."

But she learned that Dr. Harris did not respond as did other men. Not that she thought he was queer. Maybe it was just a matter of the cook having no appetite. If you spent all day talking about sex you probably wanted to paint watercolors on your day off.

"Who is the married man you love?"

"We work in the same office."

"Does he love you?"

She smiled and nodded.

"Say it aloud, Jennifer. Remember, we're taping."

"I wish you hadn't reminded me."

"You're doing fine."

"His name is Dwayne Navrone."

So she lay there for an hour and talked about Dwayne

but that is what she'd wanted to do. She had solemnly promised Dr. Harris that she would not mention these sessions to Dwayne but several months later, after he knew more about her than she had known about herself, he suggested it would be helpful if he could speak to Dwayne.

"A shrink?"

"He's a counselor. He's not at all what you'd imagine."

"How long you been going to this guy?"

"Are you jealous?"

He was. It was the sort of thing she stored up so she could tell Dr. Harris the next week.

"What do you tell him?"

"How impotent you are. How you never want to make love."

The next half-hour was frantic but afterward, lying on his back, he said, "I feel the guy's in bed with us."

Jennifer decided she wouldn't mention that to Dr. Harris.

The infuriating thing was that after he did meet with Harris he wouldn't tell her about it.

"You know the rules, Jennifer."

Now she felt that Harris was somehow getting between her and Dwayne. She had always kept rigidly separated the version of their affair she gave Harris and the reality of the thing. The reality was that she wanted Dwayne to marry her. There were lots of theories about the modern woman and Jennifer had tried to adopt some of them. But when all was said and done she wanted a man to support her, give her a house, make her large with child, cherish her. Very old fashioned. Very consistent with the girl who wanted to model and stare wide-eyed from the glossy pages of fashion magazines.

The problem was that Dwayne had a wife and she never let him forget it.

"Hey, if I want nagging, I can get it at home."

She flicked him with her nails. "You can take that home too."

Was it only her body he wanted, those wild hours in her bed on West 12th Street? It didn't sound like he was much of a husband to his present wife. Mavis. What kind of name is that? She had no reason to think he could be transformed into the kind of husband she now knew she wanted. Maybe Mavis hadn't worked on him enough despite the recurrent gripe about how he got nagged at home. Lately though his manner gave her hope. He made mysterious remarks about their future and things had been looking good. Until today. Today he had really crashed.

"A friend of my wife's disappeared from work."

"Disappeared."

"They think she was kidnapped."

"Good Lord."

They looked across the intervening distance at one another as they talked by phone. Dwayne looked busy and so did she. Who would think they were talking to a fellow employee across the room?

"She's all upset."

"I don't blame her."

"She thinks they were after her."

That was the remark she remembered later, at home, alone, all but overcome with the feeling that everything that had happened in recent months converged on today and could be summed up in that one remark.

"She thinks they were after her."

14

"What shall we do?"

Dwayne was home but Mavis wasn't there so he had answered the phone and heard Harris's voice.

"You really goofed."

"Uh uh. You goofed. We got the lady carrying the purse you described."

"You were supposed to take care of a lady, not a purse. You goofed."

The silence went on for a full minute but Dwayne waited. He knew the kind of games Harris liked to play. The stupid ass had kidnapped Gloria Sheahan, which hadn't been the deal at all, and Dwayne was damned if he was going to take the blame for the mistake. Or pay for it.

"We can't just put her back and start over."

"Let her go."

"You're as bad as Ruffle. He says we should strip her and release her naked on a country road."

"What's wrong with that?"

"You are devoid of the milk of human kindness. I suggest a swift and sure execution and a clean slate."

Dwayne was shaking his head as he listened. "Listen and listen good. Deal me out as of right now. Understand? There's no way we can go on from here. You got trouble, you take care of that any way you like, but our deal is off."

He put the phone down gently and felt suffused with righteousness. For weeks he had been living with the realization that he had arranged for his wife's death. No matter all the bullshit Harris had given him, that was wrong, murder, and made much worse because this was a woman he had married. You had to be tilted in Harris's Lazy Boy to think killing your wife was just an option you faced and one which, appropriately considered, was legitimate.

When the phone began to ring, he looked at it but did not answer. Harris was a persistent man and Dwayne did not want to push his luck by talking to him again. Before he knew it the guy would have talked him into something he did not want to be talked into. But then the thought of the money he had already given Harris came and he picked up the phone.

"Dwayne?"

"Who's that?"

"Henny. You heard what happened to Gloria?"

"The poor kid."

"The cops flagged me down when I was coming from the track. Hey, what're you doing now?"

Waiting for his wife to come home. But it was now after seven and there was no Mavis, no indication where she was or when she would be home. He would feel ridiculous calling the police and asking if they knew where his wife was.

"What do you have in mind?"

Henny had in mind a few drinks and that sounded fine to Dwayne. When Dwayne got there, Henny was at the bar, shaking with the bartender for his drink. He lost, shrugged and turned to greet Dwayne. They adjourned to a table where Henny's expression became anxious.

"You think they'll let her go?"

"Have you two divorced?"

Henny moved his head slowly from side to side. "Separated."

"So everything will be yours."

Henny did not object to this line of talk. As they pursued it, it became clear that Henny's concern was that Gloria would be released, sound as a dollar.

"When we bought that insurance, I fought it. And Gloria fought every effort to cash the policies in, get out of them what money we could when we needed it."

"How much?"

"Three hundred thou." Henny pronounced the words reverently and in hushed tones.

Dwayne whistled. "That would cushion your grief."

The question was how to broach the subject to Henny. First the prospective heir had to be lubricated with booze, and Dwayne kept the rounds coming, until his own head was fuzzy. Henny had moved into a stage where every mention of Gloria brought tears to his eyes. But he referred to her now only in the past tense. They were head to head over the table when Dwayne told Henny he had a hunch he could intervene for Henny with the kidnappers.

"They contacted me. They will again. I am under strict orders not to tell the police."

"What do they want?"

A current of greed coursed through him, but he resisted it. He would settle for getting his own money back.

"Thirty thousand. In cash."

"What if we don't pay?"

"I suppose they'll just let her go." The image of a nude Gloria trying to flag a ride on a county road came and went.

Henny swore an oath. "Dwayne, I'll level with you. I've already accepted that she's dead, understand? I can live with it. Do you think we could make a deal with them?"

And so they became co-conspirators. Dwayne allowed himself to be talked into the idea he had brought with him to the bar. He would give Harris the other fifteen and tell him to proceed as planned. He would keep half of Henny's thirty to reimburse himself for the money he had already given Harris.

"You say they want thirty?"

"If they'll kill her for not getting that, they surely ought to do it for that amount."

"I don't have it."

"I'll lend it to you. You can pay me back later."

"How long you think it takes for an insurance policy to pay off?"

"I'll trust you."

Henny insisted on making out an IOU. He took obvious pleasure in printing out this promise to pay Dwayne Navrone thirty thousand dollars for business advice. Dwayne took the slip as solemnly as it was offered and put it into his wallet. In the station when he left the train, he used a public phone and called the number in Morristown.

No answer.

He tried again when he got home.

When his phone rang he jumped. It was Jennifer. "Honey? Drive your car in tomorrow, will you?"

"Why?"

"Just cuz." Her voice like honey in her throat. "Okay?"

"At your service."

"Mmmmm."

After he hung up he tried the Morristown number again. He tried it at intervals until dawn showed at the windows. Where the hell was Harris?

15

Mavis had marveled at his apartment when Jerome brought her there the previous evening, having succeeded in convincing her that for her own safety she should remain incommunicada.

"Isn't it incommunicado?"

"Not when you're a woman."

She smiled in deference to his superior knowledge, but her reaction then was as nothing to that she showed when confronted with the walls of books in living room and in hallways and in his study.

"You've got a library!" she cried.

"Much of it came from my grandfather."

"Was he a publisher?"

"A professor."

She let her arms hang at her side, tipped her head and looked at him. "Jerome, do you realize I don't know you at all?"

"There isn't much to know. I live a quiet life."

"Professor of what?"

"Literature."

"Where?"

"Columbia." A small lie, he had been a teaching assistant there while doing graduate work.

Mavis was impressed. Jerome was a little impressed himself. Years of his mother's pressure had dulled him to his grandfather's presumed eminence, but he could read in Mavis's eyes an unprejudiced reaction to the facts.

"Where's your mother?"

"Can't you hear?"

He meant the roar of television.

"I thought that was next door."

"So do they."

"She can't really follow her programs now that her mind is gone, but it's a good babysitter."

"Is she alone all day?"

"Oh no."

They went down the hall to a room where the wizened little lady lay propped up on pillows, her toothless mouth open as she stared at a huge television set in the corner. A large black woman partially blocked her view and was if possible more engrossed than Mrs. Jarbro.

"Mother, this is Mavis."

She nodded impatiently, not turning. Jerome drew the door closed.

He took Mavis out to dinner and all she wanted to talk about was him. This was a new experience for Jerome, and a most enjoyable one. His own life took on a subdued romantic allure as he told her of it, explaining that he had gotten his position at LJCC as a favor from an old family friend.

"You should be on the faculty."

"Mavis, you know as well as I do the quality of our students."

"At Columbia, then."

She had an imperfect understanding of the credentials necessary to teach at the university level. LJCC gave such a distorted picture of higher education—at least it was pleasant to think so—that Mavis could be pardoned for thinking that any literate citizen could walk in off the streets and become a part time adjunct special instructor of something-or-other. Many of the faculty at LJCC had such qualifying strings to their appointments. It kept down salaries.

All in all, by the time they walked back to his apartment through streets oddly deserted, although the roar of the metropolis was audible from just blocks away, he had clearly made a good impression on Mavis. He had emerged from his function at LJCC and become an individual for her, one whose background struck her as exotic and impressive. Tactics dictated that he make no further overture. Had he really kissed her in his office? He threw a few things into a sports bag and told her he would come for her in the morning.

"Where will you spend the night?"

He hesitated. "With a friend."

"Oh."

"Don't worry about mother. She's down for the night. I'll be back in the morning before she gets up."

"Who's your friend?"

"Just a friend."

He left it ambiguous. In any case it was a lie. But he saw something like jealousy add itself to the respect that shone in her eyes. He put out his hand. She took it but then moved close against him and kissed his cheek. Then she was playfully pushing him out the door of his own apartment.

He spent the night in a fleabag and didn't mind it at all. He hardly slept. Before six, he rose and left and sat in McDonald's waiting for a scalding hot container of coffee to cool sufficiently to drink. It was not yet seven when he rang his own bell.

She was up and dressed and had breakfast on the table. Mildred had brought his mother a tray and turned on the television. In the kitchen, he and Mavis sat across from one another, comfortable, saying little, Public Radio purring in the background. They might have been married.

"Is this the way you always come to the office?" she asked on the bus.

"From time to time I walk."

"Walk!"

"Wearing sneakers. Many people walk to midtown from the Village."

She looked at him as if he had confessed to a habit of mountain climbing. In the office, it took Jerome more than a half-hour before he could submerge himself in the familiar routine. There were stretches of time when he actually succeeded in driving Mavis from his mind altogether. She went off to lunch before he could ask her, but doubtless that was all to the good. Gradualism rather than passionate pursuit would be his method.

The switchboard called him at 2:20. "You Mavis Navrone's boss?"

"This is Jerome Jarbro," he replied frostily to the operator.

"Hold."

But almost before the Muzak began it was interrupted.

"Jarbro? Cable. Detective Cable. Did Mrs. Navrone come to work today?"

"Yes, she did."

"She there now?"

"Yes, she is. Has something happened?"

"We've found the body of Gloria Sheahan."

"The body?"

"Dead. In Mr. Navrone's car. His wife should know before she gets the news from just anyone, understand?"

"Of course."

He put down the phone, lay his hands flat on the desktop, and stared through the blinds at Mavis who was being very patient with a young woman whose hair was dyed three primary colors and sprouted from her head like the bristles of a scrub brush. Thank God he had lent her his apartment the night before.

He remained at his desk for some time. How ironic that he should be the one to tell Mavis. He didn't think he could do it.

Part 2

DOUBLE TAKE

1

The shabby and generally uncared-for buildings making up the campus of Lyndon Johnson Community College might be merely an eyesore for the many, but for James Branch Cable they were a reminder of an ignominious period of his life when he had unsuccessfully pursued a Master of Arts in the Department of English. It was his fate to see these buildings in peripheral vision many times a week, but the kidnapping of a woman from financial aid had made it necessary for him to confront the past head on and he did not like it.

He liked it even less when a puzzling kidnapping turned into a murder with the body inconveniently discovered in the precinct.

The woman had been found in the back seat of the car and had not yet been moved when he arrived, although Winston the Medical Examiner was impatiently shifting his weight from one foot to another.

"Whenever you're ready, Cable."

Cable ignored him. Gloria Sheahan sat upright in the back seat just behind the driver's seat, her dull dead eyes staring straight ahead. The cord that had been used to strangle her still hung from her neck, an electric cord with a two-prong plug at one end, exposed wires at the other.

Cable took her arm and moved it. No stiffness. Rigor mortis had come and gone.

Sergeant Hessian was checking on the tag but the registration in the glove compartment identified the car as Dwayne Navrone's.

"Okay to move her?" Winston asked when Cable decided to go back to his car to make a call. He ignored the question and in the cloudy pane of the stairwell door saw the medic give him the finger.

"You too," he said and pushed through the door. Steps led up to street level. His car was at the curb, Fisher napping behind the wheel. Fisher slept on when he got in and called in, asking that a call be made to Dwayne Navrone.

"Number."

He read the information from his notebook, and even as he did so realizing that he was parked before the address he was reading. It looked as if the car with the body in it was parked beneath the building in which Dwayne Navrone worked. The number was dialed and the ringing hardly got going before a voice said, "Navrone."

"This is Detective Cable. I'm working on the kidnapping at your wife's place of work. Gloria Sheahan."

"Uh huh."

"She tell you all about it?"

"Why are you calling me?"

"I just wondered if the kidnappers had called your wife."

"Why don't you ask her?"

"You'd know if they called her, wouldn't you?"

"Has something happened to Mavis?" Navrone's tone of voice had changed abruptly, from anger to anxious curiosity.

"Not that I know of."

"Listen. What's your name?"

"Cable."

"Cable. I haven't seen my wife since yesterday. She didn't come home last night."

"Not at all?"

Navrone was suddenly eager to talk, but Cable stopped him.

"We've found her body."

"Her body!"

"Gloria Sheahan's."

There was an odd moaning on the line. "My God, I thought you meant Mavis. Gloria's dead?"

"We found her in the back seat of your car parked in the garage below your office. Why don't you come down so we can talk?"

There were those who would call this a damned fool thing to do. It gave Navrone a chance to take off. But it would simplify things if he did and their interview after he was picked up, as he would be, would be very different.

"You're in the basement of this building?"

"Right by your car."

He hung up. Fisher was awake.

"Take a run up to the sixteenth floor and ask the receptionist for Dwayne Navrone."

"Then what?"

"He probably will already have left. If he hasn't, bring him to the basement of this building."

In any departmental inquiry, Fisher wouldn't remember enough to testify that Navrone had been given a chance to go on the run if he wanted to. Not that Cable expected an inquiry. A kidnapping and murder were, if not the daily fare of the precinct, sufficiently frequent to move off stage pretty quickly. In any case, the focus of this investigation was moving away from LJCC and for that Cable was grateful.

"Get her out of there," Cable told Winston when he returned to the underground garage.

"Lord, by this time she stinketh."

"That's perfume."

Winston and two of his fellows laid her out on a tarp and more pictures were taken. The woman had been through a lot since she had been grabbed on her way to the washroom the previous afternoon. Her hair was a mess, her dress was torn, there were marks on her face that suggested she had been beaten. Winston was checking to see if she had been sexually molested when Navrone showed up. He stared at the ME's team.

"What are they doing to her?" He stood, mouth agape, staring down at the body with terrified eyes.

"It's all right, Mr. Navrone," Cable said soothingly. "These men are medical examiners."

"What is she doing on the floor?" He looked wildly from the body to his car and back again. "I would have seen her when I parked."

"They'll be taking her away soon."

"Where?"

He explained that there would have to be an autopsy. He had Navrone by the arm and was leading him away from the body, but the man kept looking back. Like Lot's wife, as Winston with his imperfect grasp of Scripture might have said.

"Is that where you found her?"

"No. She was sitting in the back seat of your car."

Cable sometimes read in books of a kaleidoscope of reactions racing across the face of a character. He had never seen a kaleidoscope but he thought he understood the phrase. It covered Dwayne Navrone's reaction to this grisly information. The subsequent inquiry brought out many of the things he must have thought during that moment.

He had driven in from New Rochelle that morning. Gloria's body had not been in the back seat of his car then; there was no way in the world he wouldn't have noticed unless she was wedged down behind the seat and out of sight.

"She was found seated upright. You always drive?"

"Who noticed her in the car?"

He read off the time of the call. The caller was anonymous.

"That was about fifteen minutes after I parked."

And less than an hour ago. Dwayne looked around the garage. There were caged bulbs scattered around the ceiling, the white painted walls were grimy and along the ramp were marks where fenders had scraped in maneuvering in and out.

"They must have been waiting here."

"The kidnappers?"

Navrone nodded, avoiding Cable's eyes.

"It seems a pretty odd thing to do. Put her body in the back seat of your car."

Navrone shook his head in uncomprehending disgust.

"Why would they do that, Mr. Navrone?"

"How the hell should I know?"

"It makes it look as if you had displeased them. I'll ask you again. Did they contact you?"

"I suppose you have my telephone bugged."

"If you don't want to answer, say so."

"I don't know why they would do this." He watched in dread fascination as Winston and his aides zipped the remains of Gloria Sheahan into a body bag and transferred it to their vehicle.

"They didn't contact you?"

Navrone turned on him. "Why the hell are you leaning on me? I didn't do anything. Go get the people who killed her."

"That's what we're going to do. But right now we don't know where to look for them. We will talk to everyone we can who might have any sliver of information that will tell us how to find these kidnappers and murderers. I'm not leaning on you. I'm asking your help in finding out how that body ended up in your car."

"I'm sorry."

"Let's go get some coffee." They walked away but then Cable stopped and looked back at the car. "You always park there?"

"I take whatever I find."

"The garage usually pretty crowded when you get here?"

"It depends."

"On what?"

"When I get here."

They had to wait while Winston's vehicle went up the ramp. He had the lights flashing and the siren going when he hit the street. What a cowboy. They went up to the street in silence. At least they weren't talking. There wouldn't have been any point with Winston's siren shrieking down the passage.

"Where do you usually have coffee?"

"In my office."

"Is that an invitation?"

Navrone shrugged. "Why not? I won't have any secrets anymore anyway."

"You got any now?"

Cable wished he hadn't asked that. They rode up the elevator in silence and he sensed it would take some doing to get Navrone back into a talkative mood. The receptionist was a knockout, a well-endowed blonde with moist lips and lidded eyes who gave Cable a big hello and ignored Navrone.

"Who's she?"

"The receptionist."

"Well, she's certainly receptive."

2

Henny was in bed when they came to tell him that Gloria was dead. He had gone to sleep with the conversation with Navrone banging around in his mind and had slept in the vague expectation that his ship was going to come in.

"I'll get a robe," he said, when he saw one of the cops was a woman.

"That's okay."

"No, I'll get one."

His robe was on a hook inside the bathroom door. After he slipped into it, he ducked and studied himself in the mirror. He looked like a man who had been drunk the night before. The cops were still standing in the living room like Adam and Eve when he came in tying the belt of his robe. The woman cop looked at his bare feet as if he were out of uniform.

"Your wife Gloria? The woman kidnapped yesterday?"

"Any news?"

"She's been found."

"Thank God."

He was acting in an old movie, John Garfield, being told news he already knew. From the moment he saw their faces he had known Gloria was dead. And now he heard that it was indeed so.

"I'm afraid she's dead."

Eve took a step toward him as if to catch him when he fell. Was he overdoing it? He dropped onto the couch, let his hands dangle between his knees, and stared across the room.

"May she rest in peace." He whispered this, crossing himself as he did so, and Adam did the same. Eve stepped back to the door.

"You know a man named Navrone?"

"Dwayne? We were out drinking last night. His wife worked where mine did. He called to give me support. I needed it by the time we called it quits."

"You were with Dwayne Navrone last night?"

"We're friends, sort of. Because of our wives."

The two cops looked at one another.

"What's the matter?"

"Your wife's body was found in Navrone's car."

So much for acting, Henny fell back so abruptly his head banged against the wall behind the couch. The female was on the phone now and her partner sat across from Henny.

"You better tell all this to the guy in charge."

The guy in charge was James Branch Cable. Henny spoke to him on the phone and agreed to meet with him in a couple hours.

"I'll come to your place."

"You know where it is?"

Cable read back the address he must have been given by the female cop. Henny said he'd sit tight until Cable got there. He gave the phone back to Eve. Two minutes later he was alone with his thoughts.

He went to the kitchen and made himself a Bloody Mary, then put it into the refrigerator, deciding he'd shower and shave first. He would start his new life in style. He shaved in the shower, something he didn't normally do, but then this wasn't a normal day. Combining the two activities sped them up, but he dallied in the bathroom and took his time dressing, savoring the still unformulated thought. He said again, aloud, "May she rest in peace," and he meant it. It was a terrible thing to have happen to Gloria, no doubt about it. He felt very badly about it. In the kitchen, he took the Bloody Mary from the refrigerator, added a couple fresh ice cubes and lifted it in a toast.

"Here's to you, you rich sonofabitch."

In the living room he sat in the chair the male cop had used, his drink at his elbow, looking at the drapes pulled across the windows to cut off the lousy view. The numeral three formed itself in his imagination, and then began to produce zeros like a fish laying eggs. Three hundred thousand. A nice round figure. Still, when you got used to it, not really a fortune. Say they ripped him off for half in taxes . . . Was that possible? He drank distractedly, cursing the personal income tax. You'd think that when a man's wife is murdered, the goddamn government would stay off his back.

Murdered. Wasn't there a clause in the policy covering such a contingency? Double indemnity, something like that? The numeral six formed itself and moved rapidly to the left, leaving a trail of zeros behind. If that turned out to be the amount then, after taxes, he should have at least three hundred thousand.

The net result of this figuring was that he sat sullenly staring at the drapes, feeling that the IRS had just picked his pocket of more than a quarter million dollars. It was a hell of a way to begin a day.

A moment later, he felt ashamed of himself. My God, Gloria was dead. It had been over a year since they lived together but that didn't matter now. His wife had been brutally murdered and then been discovered in the back seat of Navrone's car.

This puzzled him. Of course he was going to have to come up with the thirty thousand for Navrone. Talk about quick service? But why would the idiot leave the body in his car? Henny didn't want to think of it. Whatever deal he had made with Dwayne, he wanted to forget. There was no point in thinking that he himself was in any way responsible for what had happened to Gloria.

She had been kidnapped when he was at the track. Now she had been found dead and no one could possibly think he had anything to do with it. If there were any such suspicion, the insurance company would try to renege. That thought filled him with near panic. The morning had begun with a hangover that completely disappeared when the cops came to tell him he was a widower. The consequences of that had filled his mind for over an hour. His head had buzzed like an accountant's, or a bookie's, adding, subtracting, multiplying. The more he thought of the insurance money, the more depressed he became. The astounding fact that Gloria had been found in Navrone's car had not yet fully hit him.

Cable was the kind of guy you wouldn't believe if he touted a horse. Nor would Henny have wanted to play poker with him. The detective, once inside the apartment, looked it over as if he were a prospective tenant. Well, the place probably would be available soon.

"You got any coffee?"

"We could make some."

"Good."

Cable came with him into the kitchen where he checked out the cupboards and refrigerator.

"How you like living alone?"

"It's a bitch."

"You eat out mainly?"

"I'm no cook."

"How long you been separated?"

"It's not a legal thing. We're just trying it out." He stopped and stared at Cable. The separation had become permanent. Until death do us part. He could remember Gloria saying those words to him when they married, lots of family there, the deaf monsignor who kept calling Gloria "Dolores."

"That's my mother," she kept telling him.

"Yes." The monsignor smiled. Did he hear anything? Gloria's voice had been loud and clear and afterward people mentioned how nice it was to be able to hear the bride as well as the groom. Until death do us part. At the time death had seemed some impossible future event that you believed in the way you believed in other things in church.

"How long you been trying it out?"

"It's going on a year."

"You fight or what?"

Henny shrugged. "You married?"

"I was."

"Then you know what it's like."

The coffee maker made a pot of coffee in three minutes and they waited in the kitchen for it to finish, then went into the living room with their cups.

"When did you last see Gloria?"

Henny had thought about that. "A week ago Saturday."

"What was the occasion?"

"A niece of hers in Staten Island got married. She wanted me to come so people wouldn't wonder."

"So you still talked."

"I think we got along better since I moved out."

"Tell me about Dwayne Navrone."

Already he was beginning to feel that everything he said was repetition. How much had he told Adam and Eve? Maybe it was only because he had spent the time since thinking of it. Anyway, he told Cable how Dwayne called, suggesting they get together.

"It was a nice thing to do, in the circumstances."

"You knew one another pretty well?"

"Our wives did. The four of us got together once in a while."

"So you weren't surprised when he called?"

He went through the whole evening with Cable, carefully avoiding saying anything that would suggest the sort of deal he and Dwayne had made. The way he told it, they had just talked about the nice times they'd all had.

"Not that I thought for a minute that Gloria wasn't going to be all right."

"Dwayne think so too?"

He thought about that, on two levels. One, for the benefit of what he would tell Cable, second, to satisfy himself. What had been going through Dwayne's mind last night?

"Have you talked to him?"

"I just came from there."

"What did he say?"

"He's as surprised as anyone her body was found in his car. She wasn't there when he drove in."

"Funny he drove."

"Wasn't that usual?"

"Are you kidding? With parking fees what they are, to say nothing of traffic in and out. You get on a train in New Rochelle, get out at Grand Central and walk a few blocks. No sweat. Why drive?"

3

"Mavis? Dwayne. Have you heard?"

"What?"

"They found Gloria."

"Oh my God."

"Mavis, they found her body in the back seat of our car."

"In New Rochelle!"

"No, no. In town. I drove in today and not long after I got upstairs, someone reported a dead woman sitting in the back seat of the car."

Across the desk a young woman with the fine features of an Ethiopian sat patiently, her back ramrod straight, her exquisite head immobile atop the graceful column of her throat. Mavis told Dwayne to hold.

"I am going to have to turn you over to another advisor. An emergency has arisen." She nodded toward the phone. The great eyes followed her gesture with an incomprehension millennia of folk wisdom did not diminish. Mavis rose and waited for the woman to get up, then took her into Jerome.

"Dwayne's on the line, they've found Gloria, could you please take care of . . ."

The regal woman was telling Jerome her name when Mavis fled back to her desk.

"Dwayne?"

"That's about it. The police came and I talked with them. It's pretty goddamn embarrassing telling people you don't know how a dead body got into your car."

"How awful. Poor, poor Gloria. Did they say how she died?"

"They were examining the body when I went down to the garage. They seemed to think she was raped."

A cry escaped Mavis's mouth. "Who in the name of God would do such a thing?"

A stupid question. One lived in a world where just such things were liable to happen at any moment. Sex-crazed men roamed the city, rape was everywhere, condoms were dispensed in grade schools, the world had gone mad. The simplest and least irrational explanation of the kidnapping was rape. Men lurking in the stairwell, ready to grab any female who went by and take her away for some awful orgy. What had Gloria gone through before they killed her? Mavis was crying now, a steady despairing flow of tears that turned the office into Sea World.

"Does Henny know?"

"I suppose. I went out with him last night."

"No wonder I couldn't reach you." She crossed her legs as well as her fingers as she told this lie. "I stayed with a girl from the office. I was pretty upset and then when I couldn't reach you . . ."

How easy it was to deceive him. From the moment she woke up she had been rehearsing what she would say to Dwayne to explain the fact that she had not come home all night. They had never spent a night apart before and when she first heard his voice she had assumed he was calling to ask where she'd been. Then the Ethiopian student had seemed a good excuse to keep the conversation short.

"Tell me about the police."

It seemed unfair that after she had spent the night in Jerome's apartment and felt guilty as sin about it, although of course nothing at all had happened, it should be Dwayne who was all but accused of having something to do with Gloria's death. That was ridiculous, of course, Dwayne hardly knew either Gloria or Henny. But how in the world had Gloria's body ended up in the back seat of Dwayne's car?

"I can't understand why you drove today."

"It was an impulse."

"You never had it before."

"I never spent the night alone before."

"What time did you get home?"

"I might just as well have stayed out all night."

"It sounds like you almost did. How was Henny?"

"What difference does it make? Last night we thought she was still alive."

"I hope he didn't pretend to be all broken up. He moved out on her, you know."

"We talked about that."

"Oh?"

"It was just an experiment. They fought, who doesn't, and they decided absence might make the heart grow fonder. It was kind of like you not coming home last night."

"Are you trying to make me feel guilty because I accepted an offer to avoid the ride to New Rochelle after the strangest day I have ever lived through in all my life?"

"Who'd you stay with?"

"You don't know her."

"I hope you don't intend to make this a habit."

"Dwayne." Obviously he was taking her not coming home harder than he had at first pretended. "You're just edgy from talking to the police. Why would they put her body in your car?"

"The police?"

"The kidnappers. Like you said, they must have been lurking in the garage when you parked."

"Maybe they just picked a car at random. They had a body to get rid of and I must have left the back door unlocked."

"What did the police make of it?"

"Did you meet a detective named Cable?"

"Of course. He's in charge."

"He's a suspicious sonofabitch."

"It's his job."

"Speaking of jobs, I better get back to mine."

"Me too."

The Ethiopian was still with Jerome after she hung up. Mavis brought a game program up on the screen and spent a mindless ten minutes zapping parachutists. On the periphery of her mind, she went over the call from Dwayne. If what he said Cable told him was true, it did look as if someone had a grudge against him, putting Gloria's body in his car like that. Pointing the finger? But no one would believe Dwayne had driven to work with a dead body in the back seat. Of course the police would have to question him and superficially it did look suspicious, but finally it came down to the fact that someone for whatever reason had put Gloria's body in Dwayne's car.

A random choice? That seemed very unlikely, but if it was on purpose and if it couldn't be taken seriously as an attempt to implicate Dwayne it at least showed that the kidnapper knew who Dwayne was, the husband of the woman they had meant to kidnap. She shuddered at the thought that she might have gone through the ordeal Gloria had gone through, the terror of being grabbed as she walked down the hall, subject to repeated rape—it seemed clear to Mavis that maniacs like this would take their pleasure a multitude of times. How many were there? Poor Gloria.

The Ethiopian was on her feet now. Mavis got the game off the screen. She had to tell Jerome these latest developments. Her phone rang and she had half a mind to ignore it, but finally she picked it up and heard the voice she had heard the previous morning.

"You're next."

4

Jennifer spent the morning dodging Dwayne. How could she explain to him her request that he drive in today from New Rochelle when the result had been the placing of the dead body of that poor woman in the back seat of his car? If she told him Dr. Harris had told her to do it he would probably think Harris had something to do with the dead woman and that was silly.

Dwayne was on his feet again and Jennifer beat it to the ladies' room. She felt she had spent most of the morning in there. This time she brought her book, a fat paperback two inches thick with a red and gold cover that depicted a young woman being ravished by a very determined man with a cleft chin. For three hundred pages the couple had been on the verge of going to bed; Florence the heroine had now recognized the silent Ballentine as a gentleman, in line for a title and fortune who, if he could extricate himself from an arranged unwanted engagement, would certainly ask her addled aunt for Florence's hand. Jennifer sometimes found such stories far more real than the world in which she lived.

Her modeling career that never was, working here, pouring out her soul to Dr. Harris, sleeping with Dwayne once a week, what did it all add up to? The fictional Florence had a possible future with Ballentine to look forward to, but what lay in store for Jennifer Bailey?

Her horoscope that morning had been tantalizing: *A great change awaits you. After a period of aching sadness, your heart's desire will be granted.*

Jennifer didn't like the suggestion that sadness lay in wait for her. It was as difficult to imagine what could go wrong with her life as it was to say what her heart's desire was. It had been modeling, but she knew she could not go back to that. Was Dwayne her heart's desire? Did she want him every day, forever and ever? Up until this morning she would have answered yes without hesitation. It had been a shock seeing the way that detective had grilled Dwayne. Jennifer would not want a detective poking into her life.

Had Dwayne told the man that he had driven his car that morning because Jennifer asked him to? If he had, he would have needed a plausible reason why he should get a call from her as well as say what her reason had been. Jennifer found herself wanting to know how he had answered the questions. If she knew why he thought she had asked it might help her to form a plausible story.

"Why did you telephone Mr. Navrone and urge him to drive his car today?"

She put this question to herself in the john, leaning toward the mirror to smooth the eyeshadow on her right lid. She had no answer. She could tell the truth, of course, but that would be harder to explain than the fact that she couldn't explain why she had called Dwayne. On the other hand, this could be a golden opportunity to let people know about her and Dwayne. Jennifer was certain no one in the office had the slightest suspicion about them.

She stepped back from the mirror so that by turning she could get a full view of herself. She liked what she saw. More important, she knew Dwayne liked her. What did a woman have besides her looks and her body? Dwayne liked her looks and he knew all about her body. Had she squandered a chance to pry him loose from his wife to become her support and beloved? Playing coy had never been her strong suit. The more she thought of it, using the investigation of the death of that poor woman as a means of making public her affair with Dwayne seemed the chance of a lifetime.

She thought of her horoscope.

A great change awaits you. After a period of aching sadness, your heart's desire will be granted.

It cast little light on her situation. Small wonder. She wrote them herself then sealed them in small envelopes, dates written on them, messages addressed to her future self, the Jennifer who would exist a month or so hence. She tried always to have a cushion of three weeks' worth of good and bad luck signed and sealed and ready to be read on the appropriate day.

"Read my foot," Dwayne had said the first time she offered to read his palm. She ran her index finger from toes to heel and he surrendered his palm.

"You have a long life line."

"Not at the moment."

"I'm serious. Palmology is an ancient science."

His hand proved to be uninteresting, but of course she did not tell him that. She decided against Tarot cards.

It occurred to her in the ladies' that her concern about the future had given her no inkling of this dreadful murder that somehow concerned her. The future that today had once been might have been useful to know about beforehand. If nothing else she would be better prepared to face Dwayne. But most days were simply what they were, neither interesting nor the reverse. To have been able to predict them would mean nothing. Even her forged horoscopes were intentionally vague, meant to accommodate almost anything.

"You set me up," Dwayne said, grabbing her arm before she could slip back into the ladies' again.

"You're hurting my arm."

"You asked me to drive today and fifteen minutes after I get here a body is put in my car. Where did you get her?"

"Where did I get her?"

"Let's go to lunch."

The lunchroom was on the floor above. They took the stairway, skipping up the stairs in silence, she to keep ahead of him, he to pin her down at last. They pushed trays through the line but she took only a Jell-O salad and coffee. He sat across from her, ignoring his tray of food.

"When I tell them why I drove today they will ask you why you urged me to bring my car. I want to hear the answer before you tell them."

"I will deny asking you to drive."

He sat back and stared at her. Clearly he had never imagined that simple lie. She had shocked him.

"You threatened me first, Dwayne."

"You wanted me to drive so you could put a dead body in my car."

"No!" She divided her mold of Jell-O into halves with the edge of her fork. "I know nothing about that."

"Who were you asking for?"

"Harris."

He looked at his tray. It looked as if he had taken one of each when he went through the line behind her. He picked up an apple and rubbed it against his shirt, seemingly surprising himself by the action.

"That's the way we used to do it. In the Garden of Eden."

5

It had been a long day. Cable sat alone in a sports bar on Third Avenue, off duty but pondering the implications of the discovery of the body of Gloria Sheahan. On perches about the saloon TV sets brought in ongoing games of interest to the clientele, and groans and oaths accompanied the fortunes of the more or less home teams. Cable's mind was elsewhere.

Whoever put the body in Navrone's car was pointing the finger at him.

The pointing of the finger could not be taken to mean that Navrone had killed the woman, unless the one, or ones, who put the body there couldn't think very clearly.

A man does not drive into the city from New Rochelle with a dead woman in the back seat without attracting attention, not even in New York.

Response: she had not been upright on the drive in, but propped up after Navrone parked.

Then, either he knew the body was concealed in the back seat or he didn't. If he did, he was crazy. Why would he want to draw attention to himself?

If he didn't, return to Home and the fact that whoever put the body in the car meant to do Navrone some harm other than getting him accused of the murder of Gloria Navrone.

The thought that the body had been put in his car in New Rochelle rather than in the garage was attractive, though it required someone to prop the body up once Navrone parked, and that meant someone lurking in the garage. Messy, since it required activities in two different places. If the activities were not performed simultaneously, they could nonetheless have been done by the same person or persons, and doubtless were.

Knowing as little as he did about Navrone and relying on his general experience with fallen human nature Cable could come up with an answer to the question: Who would want to do the man harm? Answer, his wife. Cable liked it, and not only because it had the consoling suggestion that his own ruined marriage was more the standard than the exception. He had talked with Mavis Navrone. She even reminded him of Sheila.

The Mets lost their lead in the bottom of the fourth. The reaction to this distracted Cable, but soon his thoughts were back where they had been. The motive need not be just general antagonism toward her spouse. There was an adage Cable had been taught by a sardonic sergeant in his early days on the force. There are only three motives for violent crime: sex, money and revenge. "And often they're all involved at once," Murphy had added. Even after Cable found that Murphy had spent his life in the Traffic division, he thought the adage was more than the usual bullshit.

If Navrone was fooling around with Gloria, giving her comfort in the absence of her husband, Mavis would be madder at her co-worker than she would have been at her husband. She consults with Henny Sheahan, he lurks in the stairway, grabs his wife, bags her, takes her downstairs and maybe still had her in the car when he was stopped, ostensibly driving back from the track. It is Mavis's grisly idea that they should put the body in Dwayne's car . . .

Cable groaned aloud and people turned to look at him. The Mets had just scored to tie it up again.

"You from L.A.?" asked a gap-toothed drinker whose belly made his tee shirt balloon-shaped.

Cable smiled sheepishly. It was his own footloose speculation that had brought on the groan of pain. But he had to have some hypothesis to start with. The jealousy thing might collapse under the pressure of checking it out, but he was more likely to get on the right track by pursuing a wrong one. Every investigation began with assumptions. Murphy? No. James Branch Cable in a memo to himself as he caught the bartender's attention and ordered another bourbon and water.

"You must be from L.A."

"East of there."

"Do you know Dwayne Navrone?" he asked Jennifer Bailey, the blonde receptionist, the following morning. Her double-breasted jacket showed a lot of double breasted her.

"We all know one another here."

"That's nice."

"In a business way."

"Of course."

She ran her hand back through the center of her head, a movement that should have mussed up her hair-do but seemed to be a necessary condition of it. "Wasn't it awful, finding a body in his car."

"What do you make of that?"

"She was kidnapped, wasn't she?"

"I guess you could say that."

"What would you say?"

"No ransom was asked for."

Her plush lips rounded in surprise. "Then what was the point?"

"There are a lot of maniacs running around."

She thought about that. "I guess you'd have to be nuts to put a dead body in somebody's car."

"The question is, why his car? Do you have any thoughts on that?"

Her eyes moved from side to side as she searched her mind for thoughts. "Nooo."

"What would you make of the suggestion that Navrone had been fooling around with Gloria?"

Her mouth opened in shock and she shifted the position of her swivel chair from NNW to NW and frowned at her computer screen. "I can't believe that."

"People seldom do believe such things of others."

He didn't learn anything from Jennifer, yet he didn't think talking with her had been a waste of time. The other people in the office with whom he talked reacted differently to the suggestion that there was some kind of crime of passion involved in the body found in Navrone's car. The women seemed to have an open mind on the matter and wanted to hear more; the men laughed. A little bald man named Moran said he wouldn't be surprised.

"You know the deceased?"

"I know the survivor."

"Would you care to elaborate on that?"

"I don't think so. It's not relevant to your investigation anyway."

"How can you know that?"

"This is an entirely different girl."

"Who?"

Moran shook his head and pursed his lips as if he had just locked them and thrown away the key.

"This is all confidential, Mr. Moran."

"I've said all I'm going to."

A troublemaker? Certainly not a fan of Dwayne Navrone, who had been with the company five years less, and had been promoted over Moran.

"Did you drive in with your husband this morning?" he asked Mavis.

She searched his face. "I stayed in town last night."

"Did you tell me that before?"

"It didn't seem important."

She was edgy and seemed to wonder if she should have told him now. If she had ridden in with Dwayne there might be a way to determine whether the body had been in the car from the time it left New Rochelle.

"Did you go to a hotel?"

"Someone lent me their apartment."

The fact that she was so obviously uncomfortable telling him this prompted him to go on.

"Could you tell me who?"

"Does it really matter?"

"It's really none of my business," he said and Mavis visibly relaxed. "Unless it has some bearing on what happened to Gloria Sheahan."

"How could it? This was the night of the day she disappeared."

"The coroner estimates the time of death as between six and nine in the evening on Monday."

"Are you asking what I was doing at that time?"

"Were you and your husband getting along all right?"

She wheeled her chair close to the desk and lay her

hands flat upon it. "Look, that's enough. I'm not going to sit here and answer any silly question you choose to ask me."

"It's not silly if the answer helps me find who killed Gloria Sheahan. Was there anything between your husband and Gloria?"

"Gloria?" Her laughter seemed genuine enough. She shook her head. "No, there was nothing between Dwayne and Gloria."

"The reason I ask is that it seems reasonable to assume that putting her dead body in his car was done for some purpose."

"To get rid of it."

"But why there?"

"Why not? It could have been any car."

"Maybe. But it wasn't."

Twenty minutes after he went down to the Village Cable had learned of the affair between Jennifer and Dwayne. Weekly, regular as clockwork.

"There's no law against it, is there?" The caretaker's name was Pisgah, accented on the second syllable. His smile consisted of half a dozen yellow teeth.

"Not unless she charges."

"She could make a fortune."

"Wednesday was the day?"

"Like clockwork."

"So he was here last Wednesday."

The man's shirt pocket bulged with pens and pencils, a tobacco pouch, a black-rimmed pair of glasses, and what looked like a dental mirror. Maybe he looked after his own teeth. It turned out to be a cyclist's rearview mirror. Pisgah used it to check out the comings and goings of tenants without having to turn away from his television set. According to Pisgah there was nothing secret about the meetings. Of course no one beside himself would much care and if they went out into the neighborhood, Dwayne was a long way from New Rochelle. If they were as open as Pisgah claimed, anyone who followed Dwayne or spied on him would have found out what was going on.

What all this had to do with the death of Gloria Sheahan, no matter what he had suggested to Mavis Navrone, would have been difficult to say.

Cable knew a lot more now than he had twenty-four hours before, but it was knowledge that just cluttered up his head. The hypothesis that an irate Mavis had done away with Gloria, perhaps in collusion with Henny, went up in smoke when he learned that the woman Dwayne Navrone was having an affair with was Jennifer Bailey. Did Mavis know about that? If she didn't, it was ten to one she would know it before this thing was over with. Probably without affecting the outcome of his investigation. One more wife would be pissed with her husband, but there might be a Mexican standoff when Dwayne found out where in town, in whose apartment, she had spent Monday night.

"I don't believe it," she said when he went back to financial aid and told her.

"You know him better than I do."

She was breathing through dilated nostrils. "Who is she?"

"It's just hearsay."

"What is her name?"

"Jennifer Bailey."

Mavis repeated the name soundlessly, a schoolgirl in a spelling bee.

★ ★ ★ ★ ★

Half an hour later, back at the precinct, seated at his desk, ten minutes shy of calling it a day, he leafed through the coroner's report. Gloria Sheahan had not exited from this life on a happy note. Her wrists were still bound behind her when she was discovered, tied with fishing line that had dug into the flesh when she tried to free herself. There were bruises on her legs and upper arms, she had been struck in the face several times, the cord that had been used to strangle her seemed to have been torn from a lamp. A table lamp. The on/off switch embedded in a little plastic box still surrounded the wire. Cable had never encountered a mode of death he would deliberately choose for himself but as deaths go this one wasn't bad—until you thought of this overweight woman from New Rochelle grabbed on her way to the restroom and put through a series of horrors that ended in her death. Why?

The dirt on Gloria's knees and clothing, particularly her shoes, was being examined to see if it would give any lead to where she had spent the four to seven hours from her capture to her death. She had not been sexually molested. If she had been, the hypothesis that she had just been grabbed by a couple of horny rapists would have appealed. Cable was glad that was ruled out. It might yet turn out that there was neither rhyme nor reason to this killing but it was both his job and his disposition to resist that. Of course, even if there was an explanation, it did not follow that he would discover it before his superiors decided that his time could be better spent on another crime.

From the precinct he went to the sports bar and from there he would go home. He would dine on pizza, coleslaw, and beer, alone in his apartment, Dave Brubeck's trio filling the place with jazz; he would try to ignore the life he led.

What if he had met the pitiful requirements of LJCC, gotten an M.A., gotten into NYU on the strength of that, and ended up teaching English? If the position were at LJCC it was difficult to think of it as attractive. What was attractive was what had drawn him to graduate studies in the first place: books. His apartment was full of them, piled, stacked, strewn, some on shelves. It was his books as much as anything that had caused Sheila to leave him. He decided he would go home and eat and then settle down with *The Anatomy of Melancholy*. He had bought it during his first semester at LJCC. That had been before Mavis and Gloria had gone to work in financial aid, but presumably Jerome Jarbro was already in place.

He called the precinct from the sports bar, just for the hell of it, because he had the odd feeling they were trying to reach him. They were. He ran out to his car.

6

Tuesday night Jerome slept in the same bed, between the same sheets, as Mavis had the night before, and was as thrilled as an adolescent or fetishist by the thought. All day Tuesday he had sought an opportunity to talk with her, to get her alone as they had been alone in his office Monday afternoon when he offered his apartment as refuge. He waited in vain for some sign that she had regarded her overnight stay in his apartment as he himself did. But her husband was suddenly caught up in a horrible plight when Gloria's body was discovered in his car. Jerome offered his shoulder to lean on, but Mavis did not respond. It was inescapable that she was avoiding him. She left soon after coming back from lunch.

He accepted it. His good fortune of the previous day had been so unlooked for that he found it easy to sink back into his habitual sense of being one whom life was determined to pass by.

It made him determined not to pass by Haggerty's at 5:10 that afternoon. In the gloom of the saloon he found a table at which August Frye sat in splendid solitude, a shaft of sunlight alive with smoke and dust playing upon his head, a beatific smile on his face, a Manhattan on the marred surface of the table before him. August looked up when Jerome pulled out a chair.

"May I join you, Professor?"

"By all means, by all means." A thoughtful pause as Jerome sat. "No. By no means, not by all means. Think of the various savory and unsavory ways in which we two might be joined. On the whole, I prefer the manner you have chosen. Philomena!"

A passing waitress glared down at him. "Xanthippe!" he called after her. He went on, through Desdemona, Ophelia, Felicity, and Agatha until a waitress four feet high and approximately as wide slapped a coaster down before Jerome.

"What's it gonna be?"

Professor Frye answered her. "Fetch my friend, the director of student financial aid, a Manhattan like unto mine. And I myself will have another. Could I offer you something, Esmerelda?" Her nameplate read Betty.

"If you're buying, I'll have a beer."

"It has been far too long, Jerome. I thought perhaps you've been doing time for peculation. Interesting word, peculation. Do you know its etymology?"

"A woman in my department was kidnapped and murdered Monday."

Frye frowned at thus being diverted but soon facetiously acknowledged the seriousness of what Jerome had said. "Get a good lawyer."

"She was on her way to the restroom and someone jumped out of the stairway and dragged her off. She was found dead this morning."

Frye threw back his head and spoke with closed eyes. "There was a time when such a tale might have shocked or at least titillated me, Jerome. But it is clear now that we are living in the last days." He lowered his head and looked across the table. "Have you ever been to Pompeii?"

"Her body was found in a garage not six blocks from here, upright in the back seat of a car belonging to the husband of another of my assistants."

"What a remarkable sentence."

If it was a boon to find Professor August Frye to drink with, it was a bonus to have found him already drunk. Jerome was able to say anything and everything, release the pent-up thoughts of the day, without worrying about any coherent reaction to them.

Professor Frye was a charter member of the faculty at LJCC, lured from a more prestigious place by a then large salary and the promise of time for research. Only after he had settled in did he become aware of the caliber of student attracted by LJCC and then he learned that he had burned his academic bridges behind. "What was I to do? To dig I am not able and there is no room for another beggar." In different moods he identified the place with different levels of purgatory. Why not hell? "Though I suffer, it is with the hope of eventual release." Why had he stayed? Why hadn't he crawled back to whence he had come and begged for his old job back? His position had been filled and that was it.

"Have you ever thought of Missouri?" Jerome had asked him long ago.

"Not deliberately."

"My grandfather taught there."

"God bless him."

"Professor F. X. Hines."

"I knew someone at Columbia of that name, eons ago, before the Dutch came."

"That would have been my grandfather."

"That was one who was to be your grandfather. He ended up in Missouri?"

Frye had seemed to take some consolation from this.

Jerome had been a little put out by the suggestion that
LJCC was preferable to, let alone comparable with, Missouri. On the strength of his grandfather, Jerome and August Frye had become something more than acquaintances,
something less than friends.

"She slept in my bed on Monday."

"I congratulate you. Was this with a view to some more
permanent relationship, as Ann Landers might ask?"

"She's married."

Frye threw up his hands in not altogether mock shock,
nearly tipping over the waitress's tray. She got the Manhat-
tans on the table and took money from August.

"I'll have my beer when I get off."

Frye nodded, his still upraised hands giving him the
look of someone being robbed. "You have joined the
problem, Jerome. Civilization is coming down around our
ears because, *inter alia,* spouses sleep in the wrong beds. In
his prayer to be said after Mass, St. Thomas Aquinas asks
to be freed from all carnal desires. Let that be your
prayer."

He decided against telling August that Mavis had slept
alone in his bed, with only his mother in the apartment. He
half liked the suggestion that he had joined the forces of dis-
integration and decadence. He had been to Pompeii, in answer to August's rhetorical question, and had stood in
stunned meditation before the preserved figure of a man
caught nude in the baths by the flow of lava. A snapshot of
the last moment of an anonymous Pompeian, lying on his
side, almost in the fetal position. What did that single ob-
scure life mean, what was the point of it? Jerome had wandered the stone streets of the resurrected city, peeking in
homes and shops, as if he were looking back at the end of
the world. Sitting across from August Frye, sipping his

Manhattan, he found himself imagining Gloria as that Pompeian figure. If not now, then certainly sooner or later: if not by violence, then naturally, perhaps when the organism revolted against itself, cells warring against cells.

"All men are mortal," he murmured, his lips moist with drink.

"Jerome is a man."

"Therefore Jerome is mortal."

Frye had actually known his grandfather, or claimed to, yet here he sat, full of life and liquor, no indication that he was even about to retire, let alone wither and die.

"August Frye is also a man."

"And let my enemies make the most of it."

"Have you thought of retirement?"

"Such an act implies an antecedent that is not given in my case. One retires from work. I, for my sins, am a professor of literature, trying to acquaint hordes of illiterates with the great works of the imagination while not descending into their own snarled dialect. Work aims at some result. My activity is pointless. Therefore it is not work. So I have nothing to retire from."

Jerome did not push the point. He was now so situated that he could resign from financial aid and live comfortably on the income of his inheritance. Once he would have thought he would resign as soon as this was possible. After his mother went, he could pull up stakes and move to Athens or Arles or Guadalajara, anywhere he chose. The thought of such freedom made him dizzy. With it he would be radically responsible for being wherever he was. He did not feel fully responsible for living in New York and being employed at LJCC.

"How is your sainted mother?"

"Bad. All but out of contact with the world."

"Bad? That sounds like a blessing."

"Not to me."

Frye lay a hand on his arm. "God bless you, Jerome. You are a dutiful son."

It was seven-thirty when Jerome left the bar, accompanied by the reluctant professor. He put Frye in a cab and then walked three blocks, breathing the invigorating polluted air, before taking a taxi himself and being whisked off to the Village.

As he was putting his key into the lock of the outside door, not without difficulty, he heard his name called. He turned to see Mavis standing at the bottom of the steps.

7

Her day had been a nightmare.

Being talked to as she had been talked to by Detective James Branch Cable was bad enough, but his investigation seemed more an exercise in troublemaking than anything else. After the annoying session with him, she had left work early and taken the train to New Rochelle to find Dwayne also home.

"Where did you spend last night?"

She looked at him, then brushed past him and went down the hall. She had been quizzed enough for one day. But before she could close the bathroom door, he prevented it.

"Answer my question."

"I understand you're having an affair with someone named Jennifer."

He stepped back as if she had hit him; she slammed the door and locked it. His reaction had been her answer. She realized that what she felt was numb disbelief. It was not easy in the abstract to imagine other people doing what she and Dwayne did in the privacy of their bedroom. It was impossible for her to think of doing such things with anyone else. It was wonderful and frequent, more frequent for them than for other couples, from what she had gathered from gossip in the lounge. She could not believe that Dwayne would do what was theirs with someone else. But the way he had reacted to her question made it difficult to doubt.

Or was he simply astounded that she would believe what Cable had told her? Of course he would be just as astounded to think that she had spent Monday night with someone else. She turned and unlocked the door, paused, then hurried down the hall to the living room.

"I stayed in Jerome Jarbro's place in the Village. He let me use it, for safety."

"He let you use it."

"With his aged mother. He stayed at some hotel. Dwayne, remember the circumstances. I got a call saying I had been kidnapped. Then Gloria was missing. Somebody was after me. As soon as Jerome told me I was a fool to just go home where they might look for me I knew he was right."

It wasn't as satisfying as she might have imagined to carry the day so easily. Dwayne believed her utterly. His trust brought on self-doubt. She had gone to the Village with Jerome with a very jumbled attitude and there was no way she could kid herself about what had been going on in Jerome's office when she permitted herself to be comforted by him. On the way to his apartment, there had been the unstated possibility that something more than just a safe house was envisaged. Could she have been unfaithful to Dwayne? With Jerome Jarbro? The answer seemed to be that she really didn't know.

"What about Jennifer Bailey?"

"Whatever you heard was a lie."

"Oh? I heard you weren't having an affair with her."

His laughter seemed an index of relief. He jumped to his feet and enfolded her in his arms and she felt again secure in their special private world that excluded all others. She lifted her face for his whiskery kiss and pressed herself tightly against him. She began to move her feet and then they were dancing the nameless clinging dance they always did. Down the hall they danced, his lips on hers, husband and wife, male and female, and into the bedroom where she kicked the door shut and in the same motion freed her foot from her shoe.

It was twilight when the front door bell rang and she told Dwayne to ignore it. But the bell wouldn't stop ringing. He crawled over her, pulled on his trousers and grabbed his shirt.

"I'm coming, I'm coming."

She lay on her back, the covers pulled tightly around her body, missing his warmth. The voice in the living room was familiar. She lifted her head from the pillow and strained to hear. Cable! She bounded out of bed, pulled on her robe and ran barefoot down the hall.

Dwayne turned when she came in but avoided her eyes.

"What's going on?"

Cable looked to Dwayne, then answered her. "We're taking your husband in for questions, Mrs. Navrone."

"You can't! There's absolutely no excuse for this. He had nothing to do with poor Gloria."

"This isn't about Gloria Sheahan. There's been another murder."

Mavis felt for the back of the chair she stood beside, lowered herself onto its arm, her eyes locked with Cable's.

"Who?"

Dwayne said, "Jennifer Bailey. Mavis, I swear to God I had nothing to do with it."

Ten minutes later she was alone in the house, Dwayne gone off with an officer of the New Rochelle police and

Cable. She went back to the bedroom and looked at the bed. Only minutes ago . . .

She found herself wondering if that had been their last time.

Before long it was fear for herself rather than confused anxiety about Dwayne that she felt. She remembered Jerome's concern the night before. Some kind of craziness had been unleashed and she felt alone and vulnerable. In her mind's ear she could hear that voice on the telephone claiming that she had been kidnapped. And then warning that she was next.

She called Jerome, at work, which was silly at this hour, then his apartment. Long after she had given up hope that it would be answered, she stood listening to the phone ringing in his apartment in the Village. Its book-lined walls seemed the very image of security. She put down the phone, took a shower, threw a few things into a shoulder bag, and set off for the station. She would be anonymous in Manhattan rather than a target in New Rochelle.

8

Ambrose Ruffle, a priest forever according to the order of
Melchisedech, laicized, devoid of faith, disappointed in the
world, the flesh and the devil he had embraced as surrogate
divinities, brought his discontent into focus by thinking of
Calvin Harris.

His cohort and fellow counselor probably believed as
much now as he ever had. His version of Christianity had
always been its covert rejection. How could he lose a faith
he'd never really had? Or comprehend the trauma Ruffle
suffered in setting aside what he had wholeheartedly accepted as the single road to salvation and putting his foot
on the path of perdition? The last tattered remnant of the
Creed that clung to Ruffle's soul was a belief in hell.

What capital sin had he not committed? Lust had pos-
sessed him, and greed, gluttony, sloth, and pride permeated
all. Now if only as collaborator he was guilty of murder, ar-
guably the first sin committed after the original sin that ex-
pelled Adam and Eve from Paradise. Cain slew Abel. Harris
had killed that pathetic overweight woman they had mistakenly kidnapped in a downtown office building and carried
struggling in a plastic bag to the basement where they flung
her into the back seat of Ruffle's Jaguar and set out for New
Jersey for what was to be a ritual killing.

Harris had entered into a pact with a patient, agreeing to remove the man's wife so that he could marry another woman.

"Ambrose, I never cease to be amazed at the poverty of the human imagination. From one female to another. What can the second have that the first does not?"

It was Harris who had the impoverished imagination. That was why Ruffle would never tell him the story of Anastasia Foley, the widowed parishioner who had initiated her wavering pastor into the mysteries of the flesh.

" 'If sex were all then any trembling hand could make us squeak like dolls the wished-for words.' "

"Who is that?"

"A Hartford insurance man."

Ruffle's love for Wallace Stevens had survived the report that the poet had seen a priest in his last hours. Those brittle, abstract poems had become his secular psalter, a breviary in which he fed his lack of faith. He had a waking dream in which the poet came to him for counsel and he protected him from the supernatural temptation.

"Are things less real for being evanescent?"

"Memory lasts."

"But not the rememberer."

"He can leave notes for his survivors."

"Who will not long survive."

"You are fascinated with death."

"That is a definition of man."

"Who said that?"

"Calvin Harris."

"I do not know the name."

"He is the bastard who shot at me as I fled from the cottage near Morristown. A bullet might have struck me."

Harris had said he aimed at the ground behind, as police

control rioters, but the likelihood was that bullets would carom off the street and into the legs of the demonstrators. Harris took refuge in the fact that he was a bad shot.

"That is the first time I ever fired a weapon."

"My God."

Beginning golfers shoot holes in one. He was lucky indeed that Harris had not gunned him down whatever his intention might have been.

After Harris went back inside, Ruffle crept back to his car and slipped in beside the wheel. The Jaguar was noiseless as he started the engine. He eased out of the yard and down the dirt road to the county highway.

Thus he had left the priesthood, without fanfare, slipping away like a thief in the night, letting the parishioners and eventually the bishop figure out what had happened. He changed his name; his appearance changed under the riotous living that characterized his first year of freedom. Once he telephoned Anastasia Foley, but going back to her would have been like moving into the rectory again. He eased the instrument back into its cradle, writing a definitive *finis* to his priestly past. He had been married two months to a former nun who was crazed with sex and whom he had abandoned without forewarning. He told Harris he was divorced.

He had first met Harris in the washroom where he had gone to surprise himself in the mirror the better to assess the beard he was growing. A key in the lock, then the entry of Calvin Harris. Ruffle introduced himself to this putative fellow occupant of the building. Harris locked himself into a stall as he continued his self-identification. Ruffle waited through the rumblings indicative of healthy bowels that punctuated remarks lofted over the ebony marble sides of the stall. From the beginning, Harris had put him in demeaning positions. What would the future have been like if that day he had simply returned to his office, leaving Harris to waste his sweetness on the deserted air of the washroom?

With obvious pride, Harris showed him his consulting rooms. One was leather and dark wood with gilt framed oils of dusky country scenes; the other was all bright pastels, steel, and pictures of nothing in particular rendered in inoffensive colors.

"Men and women?"

"You disappoint me."

It pleased Harris to be disappointed by Ruffle. A huge Bible lay upon his desk. A prop?

"My dear fellow, civilization as we know it is unintelligible apart from that book."

"Civilization and its discontents?"

"I am a Jungian."

His own approach might be dubbed Ligourian. He used the same techniques he had used as a confessor, suitably altered. Once he had absolved from sin penitents who felt remorse and contrition for what they had done. Now he enabled a troubled person to rediscover his essential innocence. Failing to meet standards of one's own invention should not be productive of guilt. When a patient arose, her session finished, he felt the same satisfaction he had in the moment after absolving a penitent and sliding shut the grille. But his clients could not possibly feel the relief his parishioners had. There was no clinical counterpart to absolution from sin. Still, one did what one could. Ruffle had a modest but growing practice and had fashioned a satisfying *modus vivendi,* and then Harris arrived.

"We are charlatans, of course."

"We were charlatans. I got over it."

"I was never ordained. Admit you're not sincere.

Ambrose, life is only tolerable when seen as a dream within a dream, a lie within a lie. Last night I spent three hours pouring over NASA photographs of Mars."

"Le silence de ces espaces infinis m'effroie. "

"Who's that?"

"Maurice Chevalier." What had Harris studied in the seminary?

"The human heart, Ambrose. This accidentally arisen, infinitely complex, perfectly predictable product of evolution we call the human heart."

"You don't believe in evolution."

"Believe in it is all I can do. It is our myth, more incredible than Genesis, resistant to all counterevidence, eternal truth."

"You exploit your patients."

"And you are trying mine. Ambrose, your shock is shocking. Of course I exploit them. I am the instrument of their self-delusion. I am whatever they want me to be."

"I hope you don't have any suicidal patients."

Harris smiled slyly. That was the great watershed of their friendship which came from being professional, a chance result of their being in the same building, became a collaboration Ambrose would once have called diabolical. Harris defied him to find a rationally convincing argument against acting as he did.

"Ambrose, if someone wants to shuffle off this mortal coil, really wants to, withstands all considerations as to an alternative decision, that someone has a right to bid the world adieu."

"But not a right to our cooperation."

"If you mean we have no duty to help, I agree. I am free in the matter. But I am free to help."

Would the devil fail to recognize quotations from Pascal

or the poetry of Wallace Stevens? Perhaps. Omniscience was a divine, not a satanic, property. Thinking of Harris as a devil in the world, his body a convincing phantasm, his mission to capture souls for hell, came easily. Cooperation with him became a pact with the devil.

That was why when Ruffle drove away from the cottage he was making a decision that set his heart to singing. He sang aloud all the way back to Manhattan, intoning a Lamentation from Tenebrae as he whooshed through the tunnel. *De lamentatione Ieremiae prophetae. Jerusalem, Jerusalem, convertere ad Dominum Deum tuum.* He dined out, doing away with a bottle of Barolo, went to bed early and slept the sleep of the just. When he phoned down on the next morning to have his Jaguar brought to the front door he was told it was not in the garage.

"I put it there myself last night."

"It's not there now."

"I'll be down."

His parking space was not just an absence of car, but a privation. It looked like a socket whose tooth is missing. It was only then that he told himself it was Harris, but he had subconsciously known this since calling the garage and receiving the unnerving response.

"Are you saying it's stolen?"

"Not until I check something."

He took a cab to his office, but did not go up. The Jaguar stood in his parking space. It looked marvelous. There were signs that it had been washed since last night. He circled it and found nothing out of line. Just a practical joke. Or so it seemed until, just to be thorough, he opened the trunk.

9

Not until he found the small puncture on her inner arm did Winston the coroner know how the blonde had died. Even in death, she was beautiful.

"I don't blame you for not hurrying," Cable murmured through his mask.

"Necrophilia does not become you, Cable."

Nor mourning either, but he felt an inexpressible sadness standing smocked and masked, watching Winston make a prolonged preliminary examination. As soon as he reached for knife or saw, Cable was out of there. There wasn't a mark on the body, except the all but invisible puncture mark.

"Poison?"

"Perhaps the poison we breathe. And I do not speak as a tree hugger. Air. Oxygen. That's a vein."

Each of the four elements can be lethal under certain circumstances, but air seemed the most innocuous of all. Fire was a *prima facie* menace; earth and water can suffocate, but air? Nonetheless, let just so much be introduced into the bloodstream and death was inevitable.

"And cheap."

"She could have done it herself?"

"Uh uh."

126

"Why not?"

This time Navrone's car had been parked in his driveway in New Rochelle when a passing jogger noticed the naked blonde in the back, seated just behind the driver's seat. He approached the car on tiptoe, as if his sneakers might wake the dead. When he shook the car, to get the nude woman's attention, she fell slowly onto her side. The jogger made the phone call from a deli at the end of the block. Cable explained this to Winston.

"No needle in the car?"

"Not a stitch of clothing either."

"We got jurisdiction in New Rochelle?"

"They're happy to have us do their work. Besides, it looks like a single case."

"She wasn't married?"

How can you tell when a masked man is smiling? The eyes.

Navrone had put up a physical fight in the driveway when he was taken out of the house to see the body. Again he denied having anything to do with it.

"You knew Gloria. You knew Jennifer."

"Jennifer, yes. Not Gloria." He glanced toward the house. "God damn it, Cable, I loved that woman. Not like my wife, but I loved her."

He wore a ravaged look as he stared at her staring down the street of nothingness. They had tipped her up again so the jogger could verify that that's the way he had first seen her, and she stayed up.

"How did she die?"

"It's hard to say."

"Maybe she had a heart attack." Hope leapt in his voice.

"Did she have a weak heart?"

"Not in that sense."

Cable told himself Navrone had no reason not to lie; it would perhaps have put off the arrest, though Cable doubted it. He had not come all the way to New Rochelle, actually leaving Manhattan and venturing into the great world beyond, in order to return empty handed. He felt like Henry Hudson himself, out here in the wilds. Neighborhoods like this made him nervous, the houses separate from one another, lawns, trees, bushes. It was creepy.

"This makes two, Navrone."

"Somebody's nuts, Cable. Do you really think I would put one dead body in my car for someone to see, let alone two?"

The answer to that was maybe. A murder committed in passion, the most common kind, presents few problems so far as identifying the murderer goes. But this case, odd from the beginning, was even odder now, and Cable couldn't ignore the obvious element of cunning. He had thought of it during the wild ride to New Rochelle, anxious to be there when Navrone was confronted with what the jogger had found. Theory. Navrone kills Gloria with an accomplice. Say even that it is a huge mistake as the phone call to LJCC suggested. The wrong woman was snatched. There is a falling out between Navrone and his accomplice, and the accomplice decides to put the body in Navrone's car. As that death is investigated, Navrone's affair with Jennifer is brought into the open, something that must have caused him lots of trouble at home. What better way to extricate himself from police attention than doing in his girl friend, putting her in his car where she would easily and swiftly be discovered, and then rely on the common sense of the police? What murderer would put his victim on display in his car in his driveway? He would have to be nuts. Navrone wasn't nuts. Therefore he would be the beneficiary of syllogistic doubt.

This had been bouncing around in Cable's head and he was accordingly surprised to find the Navrones lovey-dovey as could be. Unless he was woefully mistaken, Navrone had just emerged from a bout in the bedroom to answer the door, and when Mavis showed up in a robe there was no doubt what had been interrupted. Cable was now inclined to think Navrone was a victim of some kind of conspiracy, but why? Would someone wholly innocent be harassed in this way? In any case, Cable told Navrone he would have to come along with him, and the fighting started.

While Navrone was subdued and cuffed, Cable became aware of people gathering in yards up and down the street, leaning against trees, staring over bushes. It was like a Tarzan movie. It was *Planet of the Apes*. He was anxious to get back to the isle of stone and steel and noxious fumes. It seemed a good idea to put leg irons on Navrone as well. Cable didn't want an escort from the New Rochelle police. Besides, he figured Navrone might want to get away from those creepy goddam neighbors of his.

"I'm being set up, Cable. You have to see that."

"By whom?"

"I don't know."

"Why?"

Navrone lapsed into sullen silence. The great sierra of Manhattan loomed before them, the silhouetted buildings bright with lights, sometimes whole floors, sometimes a window here and there, some like the Chrysler building crowned with a luminous halo. The sight stirred Cable's urban soul.

"Jennifer urged me to drive to work on Tuesday."

"Aha."

"She didn't know what would happen. She swore to that and I believed her."

"If you hadn't believed her you probably would have wanted to kill the girl."

"Oh shit."

On that profane note they rode on in silence for several minutes.

"You're saying she set you up this morning?"

"I'm saying shit."

"I hear you. It doesn't help. Who put her up to it?"

"I don't know."

"Didn't you ask her?"

If he had he hadn't gotten an answer. Navrone was either a lot dumber or a lot smarter than he looked.

Once Cable had Dwayne booked and arraignment set, Preller, the lawyer that Navrone had hired got him out on bail, which was all right with Cable. He called Mrs. Navrone to give her the good news. There was no answer in the house in New Rochelle. Perhaps she had fled to the neighbors.

10

For forty-eight hours Henny Sheahan alternately drank and slept. Afterward he was hungry. At 7:00 on Thursday morning he was thawing a steak in the microwave preparatory to broiling it when he got a call from the coroner asking him to choose an undertaker to whom the body of his wife could be released for burial.

"I don't know any undertakers."

"Would you want us to suggest one?"

"Yeah."

But all the suggestions were in Manhattan. When he told the woman his wife would be buried in New Rochelle, she frostily told him to have a New Rochelle undertaker contact the coroner of the borough of Manhattan. Henny postponed this sobering task until he had had breakfast. Actually, it was more like dinner. He made a large tossed salad, prepared French-fries and opened some cranberry sauce. His kitchen wasn't much, but he managed. It occurred to him that the house in New Rochelle was his now too, meaning he had the right to make monthly payments for the next fifteen years. Unless he paid off the mortgage. What would it be like to live debt free? Like hell, he decided. He didn't want to dribble away the insurance money on a lot of practical projects. He reined in his imagination, however, readying himself for the somber task of burying his wife.

Fortunately Gloria put a contribution in the collection plate each Sunday, using an envelope from the box of them provided by St. Boniface parish. The priests were now Franciscans; there was a large turnover but they were all eager to share the delights of poverty with the parishioners, urging them on to greater generosity. Walking up to the red brick rectory Henny remembered approaching this same door when he and Gloria went for marriage instructions. The pastor then was an elderly monsignor named Brady who was more embarrassed by the proceedings than they were.

"Now you both know all about it, I suppose." He avoided their eyes and talked into the hand that half covered his mouth.

"Yes, Father."

"And you'll follow Church teaching in all that pertains to married life?"

"Yes, Father."

"How long have your parents been in the parish?" he asked Gloria.

"All my life."

"Wonderful people. Well, the rehearsal will be on Friday night before the wedding, which is . . ." He began to consult a great appointment book. Henny was almost relieved when he found their names. And that was that.

"Well, that was easy," he said to Gloria.

"He means no contraceptives."

"I know that."

And that was all they themselves ever said on that subject. Since, despite their best efforts, Gloria failed to get pregnant, they found Church doctrine sat lightly on their shoulders. Now he had come to arrange for her burial.

"You poor fellow," the priest who came to talk with him said. He was wearing his habit, looked about fifty, and didn't have a spare pound on him. His name was Bruno. "Of course we've been reading the awful news."

"Her body is in Manhattan. I have to get an undertaker."

"O'Toole," Father Bruno said. "He does most of our funerals. Would you like me to call him?"

"I'd appreciate it."

"You have enough on your mind, poor fellow. Something like this makes you think. Thank God for relatives at such a time."

Gloria's folks were dead and her only brother was in Alaska the last time they heard. Henny was from Omaha originally, having acquired his gambling proclivities working at Ak-sar-ben racetrack during the summer meet. His hegira began when he went with the horses as they moved on to other tracks. He had lost touch with his family long ago. He preferred the anonymity of Manhattan to New Rochelle but they ended up living in what had been her parents' house, until Henny moved out, that is.

He read about Navrone's arrest on the way to the track. Not much in the story but, Jesus, two bodies in as many days found in the guy's car. Not enough to qualify as a serial killer, but a good start. Except that he got caught. Well, they had made a deal and Navrone had kept it in spades. Henny felt that he had won on a found ticket. There was no way Navrone would be able to hit him up for the thirty grand. Maybe he ought to visit the guy. No, better not. How can you cheer up a guy who is facing two murder charges?

If Dwayne had been a dope dealer or white slaver he'd

be able to bargain, but murder was hard to trade off on. Henny talked it over with Gaspe, who had given up the practice of law to devote himself exclusively to the sport of kings.

"They got no case. I read about it." Gaspe worked his mouth and his mustache waggled.

"Two bodies?"

"Figure it. He's going to put two stiffs in the back seat of his own car? Come on."

"How do you explain it?"

"They might hassle him but it'll never go to trial. Someone has it in for the poor bastard. Think about it. Every time you turn around someone is reporting a corpse in your back seat. Geez."

"They did arrest him, Gaspy."

"Cops."

If Gaspe knew more about law than he did about horses, this was worrisome. Maybe he would have to pay that thirty. When he got his money, that is. The best advice Navrone gave him was to let the insurance people come to him.

"Don't call, don't write, don't apply for payment. They follow the news to keep up on possible claims. There's no way they won't know about Gloria, because of the kidnapping. Let them come to you."

"What if they try to weasel?"

"It won't happen."

Navrone seemed to have given it a lot of thought. Gaspe agreed.

"What leapt out at me from the story in the paper? The call to where the woman worked saying the kidnappers had grabbed someone else. Henny, they made a mistake. They were supposed to grab your friend's wife. What happened to yours was meant to happen to his is the way it looks to me."

"You ought to go back to law."

Gaspe pretended to throw up. His specialty had been malpractice suits brought against physicians.

"No one'll go to medical school if this keeps up. My last case was a ninety-one year old woman died of pneumonia in the hospital and they brought suit against my client as if she'd been snuffed out in the prime of life."

"Did you get him off?"

"Her. We settled. Settled! My client begged me to settle and afterward threatened to sue me for malpractice when her premium doubled. That's when I got out. I'd made a pile and I got out."

In the three years since he had been donating that pile in steady amounts to the pari-mutuel windows of the greater New York area.

Gaspe came to the wake and to the funeral Mass, which was a nice gesture. He bet Henny it would rain but paid up cheerfully when the day turned out sunny. The gloomy guy who had been at the wake and funeral and went to the cemetery was James Branch Cable.

"This is Francis Gaspe."

The lawyer and cop shook hands. Gaspe correctly guessed Cable's precinct.

"Remember a case involving a woman named Fealty?"

"Sure."

"She was my client."

"Is she still in?"

"I hope so."

"You appealed the verdict."

"Almost successfully. It would have been a travesty if her conviction had been reversed. What brings you out here?"

"I want to talk to Mr. Sheahan."

"You don't mind if his lawyer is present during the interview, do you?"

This was fine with Henny. They went to a bar where they ordered a pitcher of beer.

"Fire away," Gaspe said.

Cable did. "We found an IOU for thirty thousand dollars from you to Dwayne Navrone signed just a few days ago. What was that all about?"

Part 3

THE REMOVERS

1

"It was a joke," Henny Sheahan said. The left side of his mouth went up a fraction of a second before the right when he smiled. "You know how it is. Once I wrote out a check for ten million dollars and signed Walter Mondale's name. A joke. The guy I gave it to probably still has it."

Navrone, on the other hand, said he had no idea where the note came from. Cable just looked at him.

"Sure it's signed by Henny Sheahan. The guy's a clown. He probably slipped it into my pocket."

Cable continued to look at him with an impassive expression.

"You better ask Henny."

"What kind of services, Henny?"

"Cable, I told you, it was a joke."

"What kind of services were you joking about?"

A half-minute's thought, then Henny moved forward on his chair and assumed a confiding expression. "That blonde he was going with? Jennifer?"

"The dead girl?"

A cloud passed over Henny's face. "She wasn't dead when Dwayne and me was talking."

"What the hell are you getting at?" Gaspe demanded. It

was getting near track time and both lawyer and client were beginning to twitch.

"I'll tell you what my colleagues and I are inclined to think," Cable said. This was pure crap, of course. "The Babes in the Back Seat" case, as the tabloids referred to it, was his alone and he could sink or fall with it as he might. "We think the two of you entered into a conspiracy to rid one another of your wives. You take out Mavis, Navrone takes out Gloria."

"That's your collective theory?" Gaspe asked. "Then let my client go. Even if he did enter into such a stupid bargain, he didn't keep it. You can't arrest him for a sin of thought."

"Hey," Henny began, but Gaspe put an authoritative hand on his arm.

"Conspiracy to commit murder is more than a sin of thought, Gaspe." Cable pushed the IOU forward on the table. "I get different stories from Navrone and Henny on what this means. Two very unconvincing stories, not to say lies."

"Look, we're getting nowhere," Gaspe said. He wanted to leave. Henny understood, but how could he complain? He'd go with him like a shot, if he were free. And for maybe twelve more hours he wasn't free. Dwayne Navrone, of course, was out on bail but the judge had refused permission for him to spend a week in Jamaica.

"I can't go to work, your honor, not with this hanging over me."

"You were not granted bail in order that you might leave the country." The judge looked over her half glasses at Navrone and his lawyer. He should go to Jamaica while she slaved in Manhattan? "Or the state, for that matter."

In the event, Dwayne went back to work, on the advice

of Preller his lawyer, when the suggestion that Dwayne go to Jamaica went nowhere.

The autopsy on Jennifer had verified the theory about the introduction of oxygen into her bloodstream.

"Painless, they say."

"Those who have died that way?"

"Funny," Winston said. "It's over like that."

There had certainly been no signs of convulsion or agony. Jennifer had looked ready for viewing when they found her. Well, not quite. She would have to be dressed first.

"No drugs?"

"Not recently, certainly. I found what looked like long healed needle marks on her upper arm, but generally she was in perfect health. It's a shame."

From Winston this amounted to a maudlin outburst. Cable felt a similar sense of melancholy when he went through her apartment in the Village. It was a walkup, the unit doors like the street door looked reinforced and extra secure, but still it recalled a more innocent phase in the history of the Village. The occupants of the house spent their day in midtown and returned, sometimes afoot in sneakers, to the faint suggestion of the Bohemian that the Village still retained. Institutionalized radical chic, perhaps. Turning away from the dominant mores of the society to which nonetheless one contributed all day long.

Jennifer's place was simply furnished. It was one of four apartments on the fourth floor, two facing the front, two the back. Hers faced the street. The hall door gave entrance to a fair sized room that was a combination living and dining room. The kitchen was to the left. The bathroom and then the bedroom overlooking 12th Street, as wide as the apartment, the largest room of all. Cable started there. Her bed was a king-sized mattress on a wheeled frame, its quilt colorful, half a dozen jumbo pillows. That is where once a week she had romped with Navrone, no doubt to the background music of the traffic below. The walls were chalk white, the drapes at the wide windows a soft shade of blue. Wall to wall blue carpet. The matching vanity and dresser were old but fitted in. There was a bookshelf made of boards and bricks beneath the side windows. It was a bright, cheerful, girlish, innocent room. Cable wondered if they had any sense of sin at all when they made love.

There was a computer on the small desk and Cable turned it on and checked the bookcase. Can you really tell anything about a person from the books he keeps? There were big jumbo paperback original romances, a *Joy of Sex*, several volumes of Tagore that looked unread, at least two dozen Agatha Christies, a Book of Mormon that seemed to have been stolen from a motel in Salt Lake City, a King James Bible that had been a family bible but apparently not Jennifer's family. Her family, so far as they knew now, was all but extinct. Her father had worked for NASA but died young, of cancer. Her mother had died in a shipboard fire that broke out on the excursion she took to start a new life. The aunt and uncle who had raised Jennifer were now gaga in a rest home in Phoenix. She might have been produced in a lab and placed here in the great anonymous city, without antecedents, roots, or relations. Had the weekly sessions with Navrone been the closest she got to a human relationship?

Cable sat at the desk, depressed by his vision of the dead girl's life, doubtless because it called attention to his own unhappy existence. When he was at work, he wanted to be free, when he was free he couldn't wait to get back to work.

The apartment he lived in was the one he had shared with Sheila. How long had it been since they had talked? Sheila lived in Bayonne with her married sister and he lived alone in Manhattan, some solution to an unsatisfactory marriage, two celibate lives. At least he trusted Sheila was celibate. His own sheepish excursions into purchased sex had stopped now that the sexual revolution was burning itself out in fatal diseases. The public access station on television was a sewer of ads for what once would have been called call girls, who now offered "massage," the new code word for sex. The yellow pages too contained dozens of such ads. God knows where the supply of girls came from. Fascinated as he might be by the prospect of having some Oriental beauty walk barefoot on his back, Cable was terrified of exposing himself to disease. Not the highest of motives, perhaps, but he was in his way chaste. Looking around Jennifer's room he felt more of an intruder than a detective. What would he himself seem to anyone who looked over his place after his death?

The menu on the computer screen offered several possibilities: 1. Prodigy. 2. Accounts. 3. Diary. He typed "3" and entered. A directory appeared whose files were named by month and year. She had been keeping the computerized diary for something like two and a half years. Before scouting around in it, Cable checked the box of disks beside the computer. She had backups of all the diary files. He closed the box, returned to the screen and for no particular reason highlighted the file containing entries of the previous April. A subdirectory appeared and there was an entry for almost every day of the month, their average length twenty five hundred bytes, sometimes less than a thousand, from time to time a marathon session running to ten thousand bytes.

Yellow dress on sale, just perfect but it will have to be let out a bit. I can hardly wait to wear it when I have a bit of tan. I've never been to a tanning parlor but maybe I'll give it a try. I stopped using hairspray today, first of all because of the ozone or whatever but also because they say it ruins your hair. How great just to have my hair loose and on its own. Wish I'd quit sooner.

Cable stored it, took out his wallet calendar and looked back to April. He brought up a file written on a Wednesday.

Dwayne. The cab from midtown got stuck in traffic so we abandoned it and started to walk. A mistake. I had heels on and we saw our cab go by before we'd walked a block. Got another cab. Talk about whetting the appetite. It was great, as always, but sad after he left, as always. I've got to tell him this has either got to be permanent or stop. God, I feel like the fallen women in that novel I'm reading, lots of panting, not much else. Love and marriage go together like a horse and carriage. It's true. I'm afraid which choice he'll make.

Then another random entry and for the first time he was reading about C, apparently another man she was having a session with. Who in hell is C?

2

"Did you know Jennifer kept a diary?" Cable asked him and Dwayne said no, he hadn't.

"Could the one she refers to as C work here?"

"You've read the diary?"

"Not all of it. It's two and a half years' worth and she wrote every day."

"No kidding."

He really hadn't known this and it had the effect of distancing him from the memory of Jennifer. Until she began to talk about marriage he hadn't been able to believe his good luck, getting a doll like that into the sack, but then she began saying it couldn't go on like this, she just couldn't invest her life in an affair. She deserved better than that.

"You deserve better than me."

"Why do you say that?"

Was there any sensation quite like the pressure of her breasts against him? She said he was plenty good enough for her, then she wanted to amend that, but she kept at it, and it wasn't quite the same anymore. If he could choose between Mavis and Jennifer, there was no doubt which way he'd go, but that choice hadn't been in the cards until he talked with Harris. Of course references to C in her diary must be to Calvin Harris. If she kept a diary. Preller had told him to say nothing and beware of cops particularly when they're friendly. Nobody had to tell Navrone to keep his mouth shut about Harris. He hadn't told Preller about the counselor and he didn't plan to. Talk about a screwup, grabbing Gloria rather than Mavis. But they had killed her anyway. And Dwayne figured Harris had killed poor Jennifer too, the bastard, but how was he going to blow the whistle on him without everything coming to light? Legally, he was as guilty as Harris.

Harris had dignity, poise and a self-confidence that seemed another presence in the room when they talked. He had to have that personality to get away with bringing up what he had. Afterward, Dwayne was never too sure how they had gotten into the discussion of removing Mavis from the picture. Jennifer wouldn't have known about that unless Harris told her and that made no sense. The guy was way out on a limb, in effect accepting a contract on Mavis, though nothing was ever put that baldly. The vagueness went both ways. Dwayne could deny ever talking about such things with Harris and Harris could do the same. If he and Harris discussed it in such a roundabout way Harris wasn't likely to just tell Jennifer about it. Still, it was a bothersome thought that Jennifer had kept a diary. She could well have noted Harris's request to see her boyfriend. Say she had written that, say Cable already knew it, what did it mean? Harris wasn't going to say anything and Dwayne sure as hell wasn't.

Cable was back on the other thing Dwayne wasn't going to respond to, the nutty notion that he and Henny had made a deal to get rid of one another's wives. The first time Cable mentioned that, Dwayne was mad as hell. What a ratty thing for Henny to do, let the cops know about their private conversation when he had decided to make something out of Harris's mistake. He hadn't even suggested it until Henny mentioned the insurance money, but the chance of all that dough clinched it. Dwayne felt pretty foolish when he learned it was the IOU note Henny had written out offering to pay him thirty thousand dollars for services rendered, that had set Cable's mind going. Why had he put that in his wallet and left it there when he turned over his valuables before being put in a holding cell?

"Henny kidnapped his own wife?"

"We know that was a mistake."

"Do we?"

"Your wife got a call telling her that she had been kidnapped."

"And you think Henny made that call?"

Cable had to know his theory didn't make any sense. On the other hand, that IOU was bound to set his mind going and he wasn't that far off as to what it meant.

Going back to work hadn't been all that bad after all. It was pretty obvious to everyone that he hadn't been stashing dead women in his own back seat. The public knowledge that he and Jennifer had been lovers, far from making him an outcast, gave him prestige with other men and made him the object of interested looks from at least some women. But there had been only one Jennifer in the bunch.

The reconciliation between Mavis and himself that had been interrupted by the police was hard to connect with what had happened since. It was one thing for her to forgive him a vague and unknown girlfriend, but a beautiful nude in the back seat of his car right there in the driveway with all the goddamn neighbors looking on was another thing. He hadn't seen her since they had taken him away.

"I'm staying in town."

"You stay in the house, I'll go somewhere else."

"Like Henny?"

"I could go stay with him."

"I'm not coming back to New Rochelle. You don't know what it was like, people staring, walking by the house."

"Where you going to stay?"

"If you want to reach me you can call me here at work."

"Jerome Jarbro letting you stay with him?"

She hung up on him. This enraged Dwayne and he immediately called her back but he got the switchboard and an earful of Muzak before he could slam down his own phone. The truth was he wasn't all that wild about going home to New Rochelle himself. He thought of Jennifer's apartment and after work took a cab down there. When he was going up to the door he realized it was Wednesday and it hit him so hard his eyes filled with tears and he had a helluva time getting the key in the lock.

He went up to the third floor without meeting anyone. He and Jennifer had run into another resident only once in all the time he'd been coming here. This kind of anonymity had an enormous appeal at the moment. He let himself into the apartment and, standing with his back to the closed door, listening to the emptiness of the place, he half expected to hear Jennifer's voice. It was worse when he went into the bedroom. He had seen her dead body but in circumstances that cushioned him from a sense of loss. Now he was almost overwhelmed by the realization that Jennifer was no more, never again would they lie on that bed. He sat on it and let the tears come. Why not? His life was all unraveled now. He half envied her being out of the rat race for good.

He searched the apartment for half an hour without finding any diary. Cable must have confiscated it, the sonofabitch. He went back to the bedroom, sat on the bed, and stared at the computer.

Jennifer had bought the same model she used at work. Dwayne had never seen this one in use. He went to the desk, switched it on, saw the menu and pulled out a chair and sat. In a moment, he was browsing through the diary. Most of it was about herself, but what else is a diary for? At first he dreaded finding mentions of himself but gradually he became a little piqued at how seldom he figured in her thoughts. From these entries, it was difficult to think he had loomed very large in her life. He should be grateful for that, maybe, but he wasn't. C on the other hand dominated the diary. Cable would have to be pretty dumb not to see how important C was and that should lead him on to identify him. When the Wednesday entries revealed Dwayne Navrone as the love of her life, he picked up the phone and called Cable.

"I think I know who C is."

"Who?"

"I may be wrong, it's just a guess."

"All right."

"She told me about a shrink she went to, a man named Harris. Calvin Harris. That could be the C she mentions so often."

"Thanks. Turn off the computer before you leave."

The phone went dead. Dwayne stared at the instrument. He put it gingerly into the cradle, turned off the computer, and got the hell out of there.

On the Wednesday morning after he had enjoyed a few drinks with Jerome Jarbro, Professor August Frye wakened with a clear head and a heavy heart. Loneliness was far more burdensome than age. If his wife Grace had lived, perhaps he would have retired from teaching and now been shuffling along some Florida shore in search of shells. For reasons that mystified him, Grace had loved the keys off Sarasota. On a table beside him, at eye level in the bedroom that had once been theirs, was a lamp whose glass base was filled with the shells of yesteryear. If he chose to turn his head and look at it. *Esse est percipi.* He continued to search the ceiling for the meaning of life. A full bladder interrupted his meditation and he threw back the covers. Esse est peepee.

His heavy heart remained after he had relieved himself and gone slippered to the kitchen to pour a bowl full of Grape Nuts.

"Do grapes have nuts?" he had asked his wife long ago.

"Only the boys."

"Do nuts have grapes?"

"Only you."

It had become their morning liturgy, through better or worse, richer or poorer, in sickness and health, until after her stroke when each morning he could stand at the end of her hospital bed and tell her the same joke, the message behind the counter of the restaurant downstairs.

"We serve flakes."

She laughed as if creation were new and she were getting first look. But she had forgotten all about grape nuts. She died, so there went Florida and here he was still educationally active, as student health might put it. He read the *Times* for local news and the *Wall Street Journal* for editorials that did not make him gag. But it was only later in the *Daily News* that he could find sensational accounts of the two murders that somehow involved Lyndon Johnson Community College. The tabloid was scattered over a table in the faculty lounge.

"There is a maniac loose," Stella Houston growled, stirring in a leather chair that reacted like a whoopee cushion. "Two women are dead, one an employee of this college."

"Did you know her?"

Stella glared at him over her half glasses as if he had made a suggestive remark. Perhaps he had. He read the lurid report of the nude body of a midtown receptionist found in New Rochelle in the car of the same man in whose car the day before Gloria Sheahan's body had been found.

He went off to class where he fended off accusations that *Huckleberry Finn* was racist. Such discussions were inevitable now. Everything was sexist, racist, imperialist, whatever. Elinora Fritz the new dean had asked him to serve on a committee to study ways to insure multiculturalism at LJCC.

"Multi as in many?"

"Surely you know what multiculturalism means, Professor Frye."

"My dear dean, I would settle for uniculturalism.

Demiculturalism. Any fraction you can name. You cannot multiply zero."

This did not anger her. He had curmudgeon status now and could say what he liked with impunity. The official line was that they were empowering the poor through education.

"To make them powerfully poor or poorly powerful?"

"August." For the dean even to smile at such heresy was out of the question. Even so, the corners of her pursed mouth twitched.

When his class ended there was a consensus that African-American Jim was the hero of the novel. August Frye went across the street and took the stairway to the third floor, stopping at every landing, imagining the bagged woman being dragged down these steps on Monday afternoon. When he pushed through onto the third floor a passing woman darted up the hallway, looking at him over her shoulder, her expression that of a terrified student at examination time. Of course they must all still be jumpy here. He mentioned it to Jerome as he eased himself into a chair. Only then did he realize his young friend was on the phone. Through the blinds that afforded Jerome such privacy as he had, Frye looked out over the busy office of student financial aid.

"August, what brings you here?"

"Our chance meeting the other night made me realize how seldom I see you. Have you lost any more employees?"

The woman he had frightened in the hall had returned and was settling at her desk. Frye told Jerome of her reaction when he emerged from the stairwell.

"That is Mavis Navrone." Jerome spoke with a reverence that caused Frye to remember Jerome's remark in the bar.

"Your beloved?"

And Jerome blushed to the roots of his hair. The woman was the wife of the man whose car had the habit of attracting murdered women.

"If he were convicted you'd have plain sailing."

"How could he have done it?"

"Leave such details to the police."

"The detective on the case is a former student here."

"Not James Branch Cable."

"Then you knew him as a student."

"I wouldn't go that far. But I knew him when he took classes here."

Mrs. Navrone had told the police of a disgruntled student who might be responsible for these odd events, a Puerto Rican who had misinterpreted her professional interest and been forcibly removed from the office.

"His name is Raul Fonseca."

"No, no. Ra-ul." And August Frye pronounced it as it should be pronounced, with his elocutionary effort blowing out the match with which he had just lit a cigarette. "Are you free for dinner tonight, Jerome?"

"I wish I were. But I can't." His eyes drifted toward the blinds. "My mother."

Having been refused by Jerome, August Frye felt compelled to find another companion for dinner. The mention of Cable suggested a substitute.

"Tonight?" Cable asked.

"A few drinks, a steak. We can shoot the bull."

"I like it."

Cable said he would pick up his old professor in a public vehicle at the entrance of the arts and letters building.

4

Sitting in the precinct with phones ringing, conversations rising and falling at cross purposes, the coming and going of suspects, complainers, whackos, and others, with from beyond, the ceaseless roar of city traffic, Cable felt as snug as a monk in a hermitage. Such chaos prompted whatever creative thoughts he was likely to have. On the desk before him lay a pad of paper whose sheets had curled at the bottom; in his hand was a pencil; in his head was what he knew and what he didn't know about the deaths of Gloria Sheahan and Jennifer Bailey.

The link between them was the automobile of Dwayne Navrone.

Dwayne's wife worked with Gloria and there was evidence that it was Mavis rather than Gloria who was meant to be kidnapped Monday afternoon.

Dwayne was having an affair with Jennifer.

Cable looked at what he had written and was reminded of a syllogism. He was also reminded of fallacies. What did those facts imply?

On the other hand, in Dwayne's wallet was an IOU for thirty thousand dollars from Henny Sheahan, once the husband now the widower of the woman who had actually been kidnapped, killed, and stowed in Navrone's car. Was Henny paying Navrone for getting rid of his wife? Objection. The Sheahans were separated. Response. Not legally, they were still husband and wife. Objection. Why was the death of his wife worth thirty thousand dollars to Henny, and where would he get that kind of money anyway? Response. Cornelius Reed, investigator for Slippery Rock Insurance, had phoned to inform Cable that they held a policy on Mrs. Sheahan.

"You suspect something, Neil?"

"I heard you were investigating."

"We've got two bodies."

"The policy is double indemnity."

"Lucky you."

"Lucky Henny Sheahan. If it was luck."

He told Neil about the IOU, and Henny's explanation. Let the insurance company worry about that angle. Back to Navrone.

If it was Mavis Navrone who was meant to end up dead, that would have cleared the way for Dwayne and Jennifer. But that presupposed that she was an obstacle he/she/they wanted to get rid of, and Pisgah made Jennifer and Dwayne sound like a couple that enjoyed their Wednesdays and that was that. That impression had been corrected by Jennifer's diary, however. The ostensibly liberated young sensualist was dying to be the wife of Dwayne Navrone. Is that why she had died? And who was C?

Dwayne Navrone himself had suggested Dr. Calvin Harris. Checking out her appointment book, Cable had found that she had fortnightly appointments with someone named C. Her checkbook cast no light on C's identity. There were cash withdrawals that might have covered those appointments, but that was a guess. He decided to call on Dr. Calvin Harris in the Phoenix Building on 23rd Street.

Harris had the dignity of a diplomat from a lesser country. He bowed Cable to a chair. Cable told him of the phone call, suggesting it was anonymous.

"Very interesting. Of course, I've been reading about her death."

"Was she a patient of yours?"

"Not exactly. My colleague Dr. Ruffle asked me to talk with her once, to verify his own diagnosis."

"Dr. Ruffle."

"Ambrose Ruffle. He's just down the hall."

Well, his office was, and Mrs. Hitters his receptionist. Ruffle himself was on an extended vacation.

"Are you in touch with him?"

"He gets in touch with this office."

"I'm interested in one of his patients."

She folded like a moonflower at dawn. "I can't discuss patients."

Cable told Neil Reed and within twenty-four hours had a photocopy of Jennifer Bailey's folder from Ruffle's files. He went back to Harris.

"From your experience with Jennifer Bailey . . ."

"My dear fellow, I spoke with her for an hour once."

"I know. Why would she call Dr. Ambrose Ruffle C?"

A smile started, stopped, then spread over Harris's face. "Did she call him that? I can make a guess."

"What is it?"

"Could she have meant Catholic? Ambrose Ruffle is a former priest, if there is any such thing. I think it's meant to last eternally."

"How well did you know him?"

"How well does one come to know a fellow tenant in a building like this?"

"Is that an answer?"

"We were acquaintances. Actually, we met in the men's room."

No Ambrose Ruffle was to be found in the Catholic Directory for the past twenty-five years. "Of course not," Harris said on the phone. "He changed his name."

"From what?"

"He never said."

August Frye called and they had dinner at the Blue Note among the German tourists, wedged in against the mirrored wall, listening to Anita Baker. Cable laid out his thoughts of the afternoon for his old professor.

"In a few days, or less, I'll be assigned to something else and I'd like to figure this one out first."

"The deaths are related?"

"If they're not I'm really wasting my time." He sipped his bourbon. "And your tax money."

"Harris sounds fascinating."

"He wanted to be a minister, his whole family was in the church. He calls himself an astral counselor but he has a doctorate from Chicago."

"He told you this?"

"No."

"A runaway priest and a spoiled minister?"

"Advising screwed up people. Including Jennifer Bailey."

"You can't use Ruffle's file on her, can you?"

"It makes less sense than her diary."

"Tell me about that."

The tourists seemed to think they were at a minstrel show and were tapping their feet and clapping their hands like Steve Martin in *The Jerk*. Cable told Frye about the diary on Jennifer's computer, entry after entry filled with superficial accounts of her day, vague aspirations to go to Cancun, clothes.

"The little appointment book in her purse is also informative. C occurs there as well."

"Aha."

"But only on Wednesday. I think it stands for climax."

"How anti." August Frye sat back, drawing a cigarette from the package that lay at the ready on the table before him.

"I'd like to find the other C. Ambrose Ruffle."

5

Where was Ambrose Ruffle?

This question first troubled Calvin Harris on Tuesday morning, not least because his old friend had not been seen at his apartment building and his secretary Mrs. Hitters said loftily that Dr. Ruffle had canceled all his appointments and would be out of the office for a few days.

"When do you expect him back?" How could he enjoy his recovery from Ambrose's desertion in the absence of Ambrose?

"He said he will be in touch with this office."

"It's rather urgent that I get in touch with him."

"I can't tell you how many patients have said exactly the same thing." This was new. In the past Mrs. Hitters had always been obsequious. Obviously he had been defined as the enemy.

"When he gets in touch, tell him Cardinal Ratzinger called. Better still, give him a message."

"What is the message?"

" 'Where the body is, there the eagles gather.' He'll understand."

"I certainly don't."

Harris went down the hall to his own offices. It had been a mistake to play games with Ruffle. On the other hand, it was difficult to take the man seriously. Harris realized that even though they were both apostates, they still regarded one another vaguely as enemies, Protestant and Catholic. And this before the contretemps in Morristown. It had been idiotic to shoot that gun after the fleeing Ruffle. He had hardly touched the trigger and a multiple burst of bullets sailed through the air. Telling Ruffle he had never used a weapon before didn't help.

"What were those shots?" his captive had asked when he went up into the attic of the cottage to see how she was doing.

"Not the state troopers, my dear."

"What are you going to do to me?"

"If you're referring to rape, relax. I have absolutely no sexual designs on you."

"Let me go. Please."

How eagerly she asked, how infinitely important tomorrow seemed to her, next week, a year from now. But it would only be more and more of what she had already seen.

"My partner wants to kill you."

"Why!"

Harris shook his head slowly. "He is convinced that all men are mortal. He means both men and women."

"You have to protect me."

He held up his hand to silence her. From outside came the sound of a motor. He hurried to a dormer window and looked out to see the Jaguar disappear down the road to the highway. Behind him, the woman was going clumsily down the stairs. He followed her down, tore the cord from a lamp which sat on a table next to the couch. He came up to her as she was trying to open the front door with her tied hands. He spun her around, looped the cord over her head and swiftly tightened it. He had his knee on her back when the struggle stopped.

The walk to the village from the cottage had taken forty-five minutes; the slack jawed cabby had been astounded when he gave him a Manhattan address. He would only take him to Newark Airport, where he would find many ways of getting to Manhattan. The rustic had reduced him to the status of a tourist. It was another hour before he was in the garage beneath Ruffle's apartment. The Jaguar was there. He reached beneath the car and removed the magnetized box in which Ruffle kept an extra set of keys to the car, insurance against forgetfulness, as he had explained to Harris. That extra set of keys was in Harris's mind even as he watched the Jaguar disappear up the road. Ruffle's silly driving cap was on the front seat. Wearing it, Harris sailed out of the garage, turned away but waving as he imagined Ruffle doing as he came onto Park.

He made far better time to New Jersey than Ruffle had, but then the traffic was more favorable. Darkness had come when at last he came up the driveway to the cottage and parked. He sat for a moment behind the wheel as silence rose like sound around him. The body of the woman was inside. He got her into the trunk with some effort, then checked the cottage to remove the more obvious signs of the drama that had been enacted there. Not that he imagined a diligent professional search would fail to turn up damning evidence. Of course it would. Here lay the real perfidy of Ruffle's decamping. The cretinous cab driver would remember his memorable request. That he could be placed in the area at all, let alone at a time that would be established as the time of death, was bad, completely outside his plan. The cottage belonged to a patient currently circumnavigating the globe via freighter who had offered Harris the use of it in a moment of impulsive gratitude.

After he had left the Jaguar with its grisly burden in Ruffle's space beneath his office, Harris had gone upstairs and lay as he was lying know, convinced that he had taught Ruffle an unforgettable lesson. Betraying Calvin Harris has its risks. But he had underestimated Ambrose Ruffle.

"Why did you ask me to ask him to drive today?" a frantic Jennifer asked.

"Where are you?"

"At work."

"I gave you no such message."

An explosion of impatience on the line. "If you're going to lie, I will too."

She slammed down the telephone. Harris put down his own. He remembered Ambrose telling him that he had been famous in the seminary for his ability to imitate the faculty. He must have told Jennifer to have Dwayne drive in. He had indeed underestimated Ambrose.

He repeated this like a mantra until it lost every suggestion of irony and sarcasm. Ruffle had outplayed him. Putting the body in the car of the client who had ordered an assassination, though not precisely this one, had been brilliant. It had the added consequence of thoroughly confusing the police. What sense could they possibly make of such bizarre events?

At that point, Ambrose should have put in an appearance, to enjoy his triumph. It seemed to Harris now that he would ungrudgingly have conceded the brilliance of Ruffle's countermove. But Ruffle had not yet done enough.

At 7:00 p.m. on Tuesday, Harris removed Jennifer's file, took it down the hall, let himself into Ruffle's suite, and put the file in the appropriate cabinet. It seemed at once a boyish trick and a move in a deadly game.

Lying on the couch in his consulting room, at once patient and counselor, he felt that he had a fool for a client. A silly pride had led him to involve Ruffle in his professional doings, a dangerous vanity had led him to expatiate to Ruffle on his theories. It was contempt for Rome, the desire to enlist even this discredited priest in his effort, that explained his folly. Ruffle himself was of no help. He was a handicap. Harris had come to think of him as analogous to the ankle weights runners use in practice, or the heavy ring players put around the bat when they take warm-up swings in the batter's box. The weight had removed itself, he should feel lighter, but he did not. Ruffle had become a menace, Ruffle far more than the benighted representatives of law and order was his enemy.

His supine examination of conscience suggested that his major mistake, an instance of unpardonable hubris, had been to put the body in Ruffle's Jaguar. It was a deed done in pique. But then Ruffle had put him to great trouble, abandoning him in New Jersey.

He spent Tuesday evening listening to Wagner and reading *Also Sprach Zarathustra*. If Ambrose had called him then he would have said that they were even. Ambrose had righted the balance.

But Ambrose wanted more. Harris heard the news the following morning in a lull between his first and second appointment. Wilfrid his receptionist was agog.

"The man with the dead woman in his car? They found a naked blonde in it last night. At his home in New Rochelle."

Harris clucked appropriately and retreated to his office. He became afraid.

This was war and he had a formidable adversary. When

the body turned out to be that of Jennifer Bailey, Harris felt fear.

The arrest of Dwayne Navrone, his client, lover of the murdered Jennifer, increased the hazard of his position. He lay as was his wont on his consulting couch, where but days before the lovely Jennifer had lain, contemplating the plight he was in, partly self-imposed, partly the work of Ruffle. He now found himself responding to the challenge, invigorated by the thought that this was indeed a fight unto the death. His foe was Ruffle; the pieces in the game, some already removed from the board, were those pitiful creatures who came to them for counsel. The task was to win in such a way that the triumph was invisible. Ambrose Ruffle must be brought down, but none need know that it was Calvin Harris who had exacted vengeance for his erstwhile partner's perfidy. He would know. Ambrose would know. And the devil would know.

In the meantime, it was necessary to learn what Dwayne Navrone had told the police.

6

The fact that she talked to Jerome about getting a divorce made Mavis feel disloyal to Dwayne despite the anguish he had caused her. Jerome had respect for her, he was sympathetic, he was a friend, and if she had ever needed a friend, it was now. She and Gloria had been close, but she really didn't have another female friend she could talk to about this. For one thing, most of her friends were Catholics like herself and would no doubt tell her she might get a divorce but she'd still be married to Dwayne Navrone and she knew it.

"Doesn't your church grant annulments?" Jerome asked.

"I wouldn't know where to begin."

"Do you know where to begin getting a divorce?"

She laughed. "About all I know is that I'll need a lawyer."

They were having dinner at a Greek restaurant in the Village. All this was new and exciting for Mavis. For years she had taken the train to Grand Central in the morning and left on the same train at night. All she knew of Manhattan was the walk from the station to her building. Jerome on the other hand was a fountain of knowledge about the city, not just the part he lived in, but the whole island.

On the way to the restaurant, he had taken her hand when they crossed a street, but let go at the opposite curb, but the second time, he kept her hand in his and Mavis, in what was becoming her way of handling this, pretended she didn't notice, acted as if it were the most ordinary thing in the world. Jerome stayed in the apartment with her and his aged mother now, making up a bed in his study. It seemed silly to think that two adults could not occupy the same apartment without lunging at one another. Still, it was odd to lie in his bed and hear him puttering about, getting ready to settle down for the night, looking in on his mother. She almost wished he'd look in on her. It seemed unfair that he should sleep on the Army cot when she had this big comfortable bed.

All that changed when Phyllis Hangar said she'd tried to reach her at home in New Rochelle and Mavis said she was staying in town. Phyllis just closed her eyes and nodded.

"I understand. And that's exactly why I called. There's no reason for you to be staying at a hotel when I have a spare bedroom. My apartment is within walking distance of the college so you can save yourself train fare as well."

"Phyllis, I couldn't do that."

"Oh yes you can. Mavis, I insist on it. I'd enjoy the company."

Not to accept this generous offer would have cast her staying with Jerome in a very bad light. Her argument to herself had been that he was her only port in a storm, but now Phyllis offered an alternative and she could not in good conscience refuse. Already she looked forward to telling Dwayne where she was staying in town.

"But there's no need for that," Jerome said, clearly crushed. "Mavis, I will stay away and let you have the place to yourself again."

"Would you want me to tell Phyllis Hangar 'No thanks I'm staying with Jerome'?" She put her hand on his. "I have to accept," she whispered.

"Is it because of mother?"

"No! I have to think of your good name too."

He nodded, what could he do, and Mavis saw for the first time how really silly it was for her to have accepted such an offer from any man. It was the fact that it was from Jerome that had made it seem harmless. And it had been harmless. She should be grateful to Jerome for that. No doubt Phyllis was dying to pump her about what exactly lay behind the murders of two women whose bodies had ended up in Dwayne's car. Phyllis and Gloria had never exactly been friendly. In fact, Gloria couldn't stand Phyllis, who was forever bending and suspending the rules to allow a student to qualify for aid.

"No wonder the place is going to the dogs."

"Can it get worse?" was Phyllis's disarming reply.

Mavis had always sided with Phyllis in this matter. Phyllis was a bit of a racist, an occupational hazard in their office. Jerome had questioned Phyllis's application of the regulations more than once but he had never overturned her since that would have created the possibility of an uproar.

"Who are we in financial aid to elevate standards when admissions clearly has a Statue of Liberty attitude toward applicants?"

"It's one thing to let them in, it's another to pay them."

After work she went first to Jerome's to pick up the things she had left there. His eyes were damp when he took her hand at the door.

"I wish you'd stay."

"This is best, Jerome."

"In what way?"

"You know."

She left him the consolation of that ambiguous remark. The scales having fallen from her eyes, she could just imagine what Dwayne would say if he saw her with Jerome Jarbro, for heaven's sake. Outside, waiting for a cab to hail, she thought of herself going along these streets hand in hand with Jerome. She must have been insane.

Phyllis's place was a delightful surprise. It was twice as large as Jerome's, was elegantly furnished and, except for its unnerving height, delighted Mavis. This is how she herself could live. Or so she thought until she discovered the resale value of the apartment.

"My father bought it for me. He called it a loan but we both knew I could never repay that amount in his lifetime. I think it was prompted by his realization that I would never marry."

"How old were you?"

"Thirty-one."

Mavis put Phyllis in her late forties now. "That seems young to decide you wouldn't marry."

"I was more likely to become a nun."

This was not a joke. Phyllis went to Mass every morning on the way to work. Mavis went with her the first time, the church the beneficiary of the generosity of out-of-towners who made use of it weekdays. There was a surprising turnout for the 7:30 service and Mavis was impressed by Phyllis's devotion. She herself did not go forward to receive Communion, being unsure of the status of her soul after recent confusing events. She could scarcely receive Our Lord when she was at war with her husband.

"You don't have to come to Mass with me if you don't want."

"It would be nice to sleep until 8:00 and still get to the office on time."

"Do it then. You deserve the rest."

There wasn't a television in the apartment. Phyllis spent her spare time listening to music and reading, when she wasn't sewing. Sewing! Mavis wondered if anyone else she knew actually sewed. Phyllis had a machine and, it turned out, made most of her own clothes.

"I love to do it. It's one of the few things I can do well."

Phyllis urged her to use the telephone whenever she wanted to, probably wondering why she didn't call Dwayne. Not that she said anything. Even so, when Mavis did call the house in New Rochelle she felt she had been urged to do so by Phyllis.

"Mavis. I'm staying with Phyllis again tonight."

"Phyllis?"

"Phyllis Hangar from the office."

"I thought the boss had taken you in."

"Don't be silly."

"Have I ever met Phyllis?"

"Would you like to?"

"I miss you."

A lump formed in her throat. "Let's have lunch tomorrow."

"What I would really like is to have you with me in court."

"Court?"

"Preller says it's just routine. But I'd appreciate your support."

She took down the information, what else could she do? Her heart sank at the mention of court. That was what she was staying away from. She hung up wishing she had never called. She told Phyllis who was delighted.

"Good. I've been praying for that."

Was even God against her?

7

Calvin Harris did not own a car. It was silly for one who lived in the city to take on the aggravation of traffic when public transportation was available at the lifting of a hand. Let the Iranian and Turkish drivers with their beaded headrests and manic eyes maneuver through the streets of a city which must seem to them more exotic than Tehran or Constantinople. He had the feeling that if he did own a car the body of Jennifer would have been discovered in it rather than in Dwayne Navrone's.

Navrone represented a danger of a very different kind from Ambrose Ruffle. Jennifer's paramour would be guided by self-interest and fear and eventually would tell the police all he knew. Obviously he had not yet. It was unclear whether he knew what he knew. Sooner or later he would mention his visit to the office and that he had done so at Jennifer's suggestion. Then he would be but a small step from accusing Calvin Harris of offering to do away with his wife.

Harris had no fear of being able successfully to defend himself against such a suggestion. He would be in the enviable position of the counselor accused by a troubled patient. And being accused when that patient himself was under suspicion. Harris almost hoped it would come to that

170

when he imagined the compassionate tolerance he would show for poor Mr. Navrone when he testified. Almost.

All in all it would be much more convenient to remove the temptation to bare his soul from Dwayne Navrone and to do it in such a way that it would take care of Ambrose as well. Harris smiled as he thought of this. How he would do it was far from clear, but that he would was certain.

Ambrose had proved more perfidious than Albion and why? Clearly there had been a deep-seated animosity there from the beginning, fueled by Harris's success in always putting his colleague in a demeaning position. That washroom debut had set the stage for a series of triumphs. At bottom of the tension between them lay the faith Ambrose was convinced he had lost. You can take the priest out of the rectory, but you can't take the rectory out of the priest. Ambrose's practice was like nothing so much as secular spiritual direction. He was forever urging his patients on to another plateau in their conquest of self. The regimens he prescribed for them had ascetic, edifying, and contemplative aspects—dieting, reading biographies selected by Ambrose, quiet times when they were to sit very still, preferably in an unlighted room, and wipe the slate of their soul as clean as they could. What happened next could not be precisely predicted. Of course something did happen next, lights, images, other fireworks as the neurons in the brain did their work, and Ambrose's patients gave him credit for what they seemed to think was an achievement on a par with the ecstasy of Saint Teresa. Ruffle himself had kept a four-volume set of the *Breviarium Romanum* which he described as a collector's item because it had been replaced by the Second Vatican Ecumenical Council.

"You miss the old church," Harris had suggested in the days when they had been unambiguously friends.

"The music certainly, and the Latin."

As a joke they submitted to one another's counseling services as the best way to benefit from the other's techniques. It was clear to Harris that Ambrose's defection was like that of a jilted woman. The institution to which he had given his heart and life had changed beyond recognition.

"The church left me as much as vice versa," Ambrose admitted.

That had been the beginning, but Ambrose was not one to go half way. A man who had accepted celibacy, starvation wages, a relentless schedule, and clothes that made him the target of every drunk and neurotic was not likely simply to apply for laicization and call it a day. Ambrose had duplicated his priesthood in his practice and gone after strange gods.

What must have been his reaction when he had discovered the body of Gloria Sheahan in his Jaguar, the Jaguar that made up for all the subway rides and walking of his pastoral life? It had been a stroke of luck that he had found the body before anyone else noticed it. Transferring it to Navrone's vehicle had not displayed high imagination, perhaps, but even that must have been in lieu of putting her on Harris's doorstep.

In search of a method, he telephoned Dwayne Navrone and asked how things were going. The man was at work and not free to talk but he seemed moved by the sincere tone in which Calvin asked the question.

"I have to talk to you."

"Dwayne, we're talking."

"Face to face."

"Professionally?" Harris smiled as he listened to the sounds of Navrone getting control of himself.

"I'm due in court today."

"Is there any way I can help? Financially. Perhaps testify, though it might not be helpful to have it suggested that you were in therapy."

"Jennifer kept a diary."

"Did she?"

"On her computer. There's lots of it, but I don't think it will cause me any trouble. You're in it as C."

"Just C?"

"Yes."

"It makes me sound so mysterious. Who is your lawyer?"

"A man named Preller."

"Are you content with him?"

"So far."

"Let me know if you should want to change. But then you ought to be out of this ordeal soon."

"I hope so."

"Dwayne, I practically guarantee it."

Dwayne had lowered his voice and was asking what the hell was going on with all the dead bodies, but Harris hung up. A plan had, as he expected, formed in his mind as he talked. But first he must transfer all Jennifer's files and records to Ambrose's office.

8

Clean shaven, allowing the gray to appear in his hair, favoring the virtual uniform of the bourgeoisie, navy blue blazer, gray trousers, loafers, Ambrose was visibly becoming his new persona. His business card read Ross Thilman, Manufacturers' Representative, with an address in the Helmsley Building at 230 Park Avenue and telephone and fax numbers. He was living on the proceeds of the sale of the Jaguar, a transaction he had conducted in the name of Calvin Harris, having signed over the title to Harris though not, of course, the money realized.

Ross Thilman was the third person he had been since leaving his parish. For the first month he had been the resurrected husband of the widow Foley since that made using her credit cards easier. Why would he choke on the gnat of larceny when he had swallowed the camel of apostasy? He had been Ambrose Ruffle for nearly ten years and he would be Ross Thilman at least until he squared accounts with Harris.

Putting the body of the dead woman in his Jaguar had been far more than a shabby effort to deflect suspicion onto him. That Harris should be piqued at being abandoned in New Jersey with the woman they had mistakenly taken captive, was understandable enough. Ambrose—as Harris would continue to think of him—meant to be vindictive, of course, he could hardly be expected to be amused by being shot at with a machine pistol. It had been Harris's idea that they go armed when they captured the woman. Neither one of them knew how to use such a firearm. It certainly was not part of the plan Ambrose had agreed to. For that matter, it was not until they were in New Jersey that it was clear to Ambrose that Harris really intended to kill the woman.

"What did you think we were going to do with her?"

The mewling sound of their captive accompanied this exchange since of course she could hear them. Ambrose had detected the sadistic streak in Harris when they had taken turns being one another's patients, but his treatment of the woman was nonetheless an ugly surprise. The treatment was worse once Harris learned they had taken the wrong woman. That was the basis for Ambrose's plea on behalf of her life.

"She hasn't seen either one of us."

In answer, Harris tore the bag from her upper body and she blinked several times and then took them in.

"Who are you?"

"Agents of death."

Her mouth trembled at Harris's remark. Ambrose was as surprised as she by the cruelty. His expression must have given her hope.

"Let me go. Please. Untie my hands."

"So you can go to potty? But that isn't any longer necessary in your case, is it?"

Ambrose told himself that Harris was being both cruel and crude as a kind of disguise. No one would associate him with such conduct. The woman wept at this reminder of her accident in the car. Ambrose had already sprayed the back seat. Later, after the incident with the gun, Ambrose felt he was abandoning the woman to Harris's cruelty when he drove out the road. He was washing his hands of the whole business. And he had doubted that in the crunch Harris would harm the woman.

"She's the wrong woman, Cal. The deal's off."

"We could drive her home and say it was all a horrible mistake. It was an elaborate practical joke arranged with Navrone and we got the bag over her head so fast we didn't see she was the wrong woman . . ." Harris spoke with phony eagerness, mocking Ambrose's concern. The woman followed with fascinated dread.

"Navrone?" she said, and ducked out of range of Harris's fist.

An oddity of both of them was that, having turned away from the morals of their youth, a morality which put the prohibition of sexual sins in the forefront, they were as sexless as monks. Harris adjusted to his own disinterest in sex by mocking Ambrose's sexless life as a subconscious keeping of his promise of celibacy. This angered him because he suspected it was true. His sleeping with the widow Anastasia Foley had been an unnerving mixture of pleasure and dread; the touch of her flesh had seemed the promise of damnation, not in itself, but because he was using her to break his promise to God. He could have been relieved of his promise, in those days laicizations were almost routinely granted. He could have married his partner in sin. But he had not been laicized. From the point of view of his bishop and former colleagues, he was just a priest on the run. Thousands had left the priesthood over the past quarter of a century and some of those who remained should have left. When he read of misdeeds on the part of priests, Ambrose felt implicated, as if the miscreants had let down the side, betrayed all those in their order. Because of course the media coverage of such events carried the not so implicit suggestion that this was exactly what could be expected of the medieval repression called celibacy.

"*In vitro* fertilization will render sexual congress otiose," Harris said.

He wouldn't let it go. Sperm banks sufficient for millennia could be filled within weeks; males could become eunuchs for eugenics sake, as for women . . . Ambrose tried unsuccessfully to tune him out, but Harris always knew when he had your goat. Goat. The sheep and the goats. The time for accounting had come and Ambrose intended to see that Harris got his just punishment. Of course, it was all predetermined anyway.

Removing the body of the woman they had kidnapped from the Jaguar to the back seat of Dwayne Navrone's car had been *ad hoc,* a way to deflect suspicion. How easily she might have been discovered in the Jaguar! What had Harris imagined he would do? Take the blame in silence for Harris's crime?

That had been the beginning. Jennifer Bailey had been Step Two. The culmination was to lay at Harris's doorstep the deaths of the two women and of Dwayne Navrone beside. Jennifer had been carrying on with a married man and Navrone had contracted with Harris for the murder of his wife, presumably so that he and Jennifer could marry. The criminal should not profit from his crime. Not Navrone, not Jennifer, above all, not Calvin Harris.

In the seminary Ambrose had excelled at billiards, the artful stroke that with carefully angled caroms effected the striking of three balls. He was engaged in billiards now. The two adulterers would bring down Harris.

9

Phyllis Hangar enjoyed Mavis's company even though her houseguest got fidgety in the evenings. It turned out that she missed television.

"I've never gotten into the habit," Phyllis said. "Would you like to go out to a movie?"

"With a VCR you could see movies right here."

"I don't care much for movies either."

She knew Mavis thought she was just old fashioned and maybe she was, but Phyllis honestly didn't see what more than books and music a person needed for worthwhile diversion. Her reading was carefully selected. From her father, she had inherited complete sets of Dickens, Jane Austen, Thackeray, and George Eliot. She had read every word of Henry James, Edith Wharton, and Willa Cather. She had wanted desperately to like Flannery O'Connor but had never been able to do it. Her pride and constant joy was the collected works of John Henry Cardinal Newman, which had been in the family since they were new.

"I have a portable television in my kitchen," Mavis said wistfully. She had been perusing the entertainment section of the newspaper and perhaps was missing out on some favorite program.

"Can they be rented?"

"It seems silly to rent a set when we have three at home."

"Three!"

"One in the bedroom."

All Phyllis's knowledge of the relations between men and women came from her reading, and memories of her parents, of course. Nothing that she had learned from these sources seemed applicable to the world in which she lived. She had adjusted to the students she dealt with in financial aid by imagining that this was a rare and tropical land and that she had come here as a missionary and would be as helpful as she could. She did not pretend to understand the customs of the natives, helping them fill out forms made her aware of the strangeness of their domestic arrangements, but she did not sit in judgment on them. This was a strange, unintelligible world, the same world, she suspected, one would see on the television. But it was not part of her upbringing to impose her tastes on a guest.

"We could have your portable set here if you like, Mavis."

"I'd watch it in my bedroom."

"As you like."

Mavis's joy disappeared. "I don't dare go to the house in New Rochelle. The police advise against it."

"Is your husband there?"

"He is staying with Gloria's husband."

"I'll pick up the television set for you."

"Phyllis, I couldn't ask you to do that. You've been too good to me already."

"Nonsense. I'll be happy to get it. The outing will do me good. Can the set be carried on the train?"

Mavis continued to argue but it was obvious to Phyllis how much this meant to her. It was painful to think that staying here should be penitential—over and above the troubles that had led to the invitation in the first place, that is.

"I'll go tomorrow."

Mavis threw her arms around Phyllis and hugged her. Any doubt Phyllis had about how much Mavis missed television fled. Perhaps being deprived of television was like being told that you would never again read Dickens.

Mavis provided her with a plan of her house, a key, and elaborate instructions about train times, apologizing all along for taking such advantage of Phyllis. She also obtained permission from Mr. Jarbro to leave early so that she would avoid the rush hour in both directions. It was agreed that Mavis would meet her at Grand Central and they would dine at a Japanese restaurant Phyllis favored.

She stopped in at St. Agnes for a visit to the Blessed Sacrament before entering Grand Central. Living as she did, able to go almost anywhere she went on foot, Phyllis found the condition of public transportation a shock. The entryways of the station were tolerable only by imagining that she was in New Delhi. But for the most part she felt excitement at the prospect of her journey. New Rochelle was not the far side of the moon, but the last time Phyllis had left the city it was in a taxi to JFK and a flight to Paris from which she took an exciting ride on a rocket-like train to Lourdes.

She carried the map Mavis had given her as a bookmark in *Mansfield Park*. Reading was out of the question. Honestly, she felt like a child on her first train ride. The other passengers, the scenery from the window, everything seemed strange and, somewhat to her surprise, wonderful. Had she unnecessarily limited her life, living in the center of the city, her life circumscribed by a tight little circle that encompassed her apartment, her church, her work? What had begun as a favor done out of a sense of duty turned into an adventure.

When she got off the train in New Rochelle, she had been given a choice by Mavis. If the weather stayed nice, it was a pleasant walk and she would get a better sense of the place. In any case, she would of course take a taxi back to the station, given the burden of the television. It was a glorious day and Phyllis decided to walk.

If living in the city had become bearable because she imagined she was only a visitor from another age, New Rochelle seemed a very different, very attractive place. She walked along, noticing everything, as if she intended to buy the whole town. She arrived at the Navrone house in a surprisingly short time, and was almost disappointed that she had. She went up the driveway to the side door and, using the key Mavis had given her, let herself in.

She stood inside the closed door, listening to the sounds of the house. She felt that she was home, she felt that she had landed on a strange planet. She was in the kitchen and there, plain as day, was the portable television set. All she had to do was unplug it, call a cab, and return to Manhattan. She looked toward the living room and then down the unlit hallway where the bedrooms were. She was dying to see Mavis's house and she didn't see any reason why she shouldn't, now that she had taken all the trouble to come out here.

The living room was dominated by the huge screen of a television set. The furniture was grouped so that the screen was visible from any chair or couch. There were no books in evidence. Phyllis ran her finger over the surface of an end table and looked at it. Dust. Her finger had left an avenue behind. Well, Mavis had been away for a few days. She went through the kitchen and down the hall to the bedroom.

The television stood on the dresser at the foot of the bed so that Mavis and her husband could watch before falling asleep. The set was smaller than the one in the living room but larger than Phyllis would have imagined. She sat for a moment on the bed. There was a device on the table next to the bed and she picked it up. She pressed "On" and jumped when the television went on. She turned sidewise and looked at it. The device enabled her to control it. After a moment, she got the hang of it and switched channels and increased and decreased the volume. Fascinated, she lay back on the bed as Mavis and her husband must and continued to experiment with the remote control.

She turned her head and looked at the place beside her. If she had ever imagined herself in bed with a man a television set had not figured in it. Of course marriage went on day after day, things must become ordinary, living with a man probably came to seem the most natural thing in the world.

She closed her eyes. The television murmured on. She searched for and found the "Off" button. She lay perfectly still, eyes closed, her imagination fashioning pictures she would not normally have entertained. For heaven's sake. She opened her eyes and swung her feet off the bed.

The man stood in the doorway of the room, a stocking pulled over his face.

10

Cable had agreed that it was better that Navrone stay with Henny. "That way I know where both my suspects are."

"I meant for safety."

"I was kidding."

"It's hard to tell."

What the hell was there to kid about? Henny's wife was dead and Jennifer was dead. Dwayne didn't know what Cable's suspicions were, but he knew he'd had nothing to do with either of those deaths. He had wiped his mind clean of his talk with Henny before Gloria was found. That had just been a try at cashing in on something Harris would have done anyway. He had too. Maybe Dwayne hadn't known that at the time he offered to insure that Henny got the insurance on Gloria, but he wouldn't have harmed Gloria himself. Either things worked out or they didn't. Well, they hadn't. And when Harris dumped Gloria's body in the back seat of his car, Dwayne felt betrayed. He'd been given the shaft before, but never anything like this. What hurt was that Harris was absolutely right in thinking, as he must have, that Dwayne Navrone was not going to spill his guts to the police.

It had been a temptation, no mistake about that. But he hadn't told Cable, he hadn't told Preller, he hadn't told anybody. Jennifer was the only one who knew of his connection with Harris and now Jennifer was gone.

If he had felt betrayed the first time, the second time a body showed up in his car he was really confused. What was Harris getting at? What did he expect him to do? He couldn't believe that the man would kill two people just to frighten Dwayne Navrone into paying for a killing that hadn't come off. Besides, this was Jennifer! God, it had hurt to be hustled out to his car and see her sitting naked in the back seat.

"Come on to the track," Henny urged.

"Why do you bother with off-track all over the place?"

"It's not the same."

"I got to go to work."

"Call in sick. You're out on bail, not on parole."

"Go ahead, Henny."

Dwayne felt he had gambled and lost too much already. It wasn't the money. The stock market had jacked up his paper worth several percentage points in the past week. He could cash out enough to pay off Harris and still look good. The sonofabitch had called to ask whether he was satisfied with his lawyer and hadn't given Dwayne a chance to ask what the hell he was doing putting bodies in the back seat of Navrone's car. And asking if he wanted to see him professionally! What the hell was his profession, that was the question.

At work, he spent an hour with his broker and almost immediately after he hung up the phone rang.

"The last time we talked you suggested we should get together and talk face to face."

"That's right."

"When are you free?"

"Now." He'd plead sick to talk with Harris, by God.

"I've had a cancellation. Come along immediately and we should have the better part of an hour."

Click. It was more like an order than an agreement. Dwayne looked around as if others would be aware of how Harris was treating him. Paula, a well-endowed brunette whose interest in him had increased when his tragic affair with Jennifer became known, smiled slyly.

"I'm going out for an hour."

"Just for an hour?" She pressed her shoulders back and looked up at him invitingly.

"I meant I'd be back for lunch."

"Is that an invitation?"

"Do you eat Chinese?"

She studied him with narrowed eyes. "I never would have guessed."

Geez. He took the elevator to the street floor, hesitated about going to the basement for his car, then pushed through the revolving doors and stepped into the street to hail a cab. One appeared like magic, ten minutes later he was getting out in front of Harris's building. Obviously, there were hours of the day when the city ran like a watch. The last time he'd come to see Harris, there'd been a chorus boy type at the receptionist desk, but today he was met by the man himself. Harris showed no surprise at the speed with which Dwayne had made the trip. He led the way into his inner office.

"You must be a very confused young man."

"I'm not a damned bit confused. But I want some answers."

"I should think so."

This was not the office in which they had struck their deal. That had been a consulting room. It amazed Dwayne that it was only slightly more than a week ago that Harris had offered to take care of Mavis. The doctor raised his brows when Dwayne took out his cigarettes.

"You made one hell of a mistake, Harris."

"Read the warning on the label of that package, Dwayne."

Dwayne lit the cigarette and blew smoke across the desk. "Tell me why I shouldn't tell the police who it is that's putting dead bodies in my car."

"No reason why you shouldn't. Who is it?"

"Don't be funny."

Harris brought his hands together as if he were going to say grace. "The perpetrator of those tasteless acts is not myself. I had a companion in our little adventure. We've had a falling out. The silly ass mistook another woman for your wife. I'm afraid I offended him when I spoke of the IQ needed to make such a gross error. For spite, he killed the woman he had kidnapped. He then went on to kill Jennifer."

"Why?"

"He has transferred his anger toward me to you."

"To me? Who is this guy?"

"It makes no sense, of course. 'O the mind, mind has mountains.' Do you know Pound? In any case, it is time that you and I join forces."

"I've been arrested. I've had to post bail. I've had to hire a lawyer."

Harris put out his hand like a patrol lady stopping school kids. "Whoa, Dwayne. Take it easy. We're on the same side. The police have no case against you. Any danger you face is from my maniacal colleague."

"Where is he?"

Harris nodded as if Dwayne had hit on the real issue. "How I wish I knew. I take full responsibility for involving him. Perhaps I should have foreseen his reaction to criticism. I didn't. But I enlisted him, you did not. The blame is on my shoulders. The question is, what will he do next? He has already killed twice."

"Call the police."

"I thought of that. It is an attractive avenue. You and I need only tell a few lies; his accusations, in the light of his clearly insane behavior, would roll off us like water. Yes, I've thought of that."

Dwayne thought of Cable listening to what those accusations might be. A lot of things that confused the detective now would have some explanation then and it might not sound like the ravings of a crazy man.

"No," he said.

Harris nodded. "I agree. It is too dangerous. This is something we must handle ourselves."

Harris turned his chair forty-five degrees, keeping his hands pressed together.

"We must act before he strikes again." He swung back to face Dwayne. "You are in grave danger."

"Do I smell coffee?"

"Would you like some? But of course you would. A cigarette, a cup of coffee." Harris got up and left thc office. Dwayne stared out the window at the slice of skyline. Sunlight softened the masses of stone and steel, beyond the tracery of a bridge was visible. Harris came back with a tray, which he placed on his desk.

"Help yourself."

There was a container of sugar on the tray. He hesitated.

"Artificial sweetener?"

"If you have any."

"It's what I use myself."

Harris opened his desk and tossed a packet to Dwayne.

He opened another and shook it into his cup. Dwayne did the same. They toasted one another, partners in crime, and Dwayne drank. A nice rich taste, Colombian maybe, and hot but not too hot.

"How are we going to take care of your friend?"

Harris put down his cup. "We're going to use you for bait."

"Come on."

"Let me explain."

Harris began with a little character sketch of the man he called Ambrose. He obviously knew him very well. Dwayne concentrated on what Harris was saying but this became harder and harder to do. He finished his coffee, half hoping it would clear his head, but instead a fuzzy cloud grew behind his eyes, Harris's face became indistinct and then Dwayne felt that he was being loosened from his skin, his body seemed like a suit of clothes and then he was enveloped by the cloud and slipped away.

Part 4

IN ABSENTIA

1

"Who gave you this number?"

Cable had seemingly just fallen asleep when the ringing phone drilled through to his mind and woke him. The woman on the line addressed him as Detective Cable and made no sense. This was an invasion of his own time, his sleeping time.

"I looked it up."

Why did the thought that his name was in the directory surprise him? The only calls he got at home were from the precinct.

"Start over."

"This is Mavis Navrone. You remember me?"

"Of course."

"I am worried about the woman I'm staying with. She went to New Rochelle hours ago, she should have been back long before now, but I didn't want just to call the police because what am I supposed to say? A grown woman hasn't been seen for several hours? I've telephoned my home in New Rochelle, but that doesn't make much sense. Anyway, no one answers, so either she hasn't got there yet or she's been there and left and . . ."

He held the phone away from his ear as he got out of bed. It was the fact that this was Mavis Navrone that mattered, he didn't know what the hell she was talking about, but she was excited almost to hysteria.

"If anything has happened to Phyllis, I don't know what I'll do."

"Where are you now?"

On 37th, closer to Park than to Madison, he wrote down the number and told her he'd be there in half an hour.

"What's the point of coming here? Someone should check my house in New Rochelle."

"In half an hour," he repeated and hung up.

The glass on the bedside table was not empty so he drank it off, mainly melted cubes, but it had a medicinal effect. His eyes felt sunken in his head, his limbs were weary, but his head seemed clear. His central thought was that he was damned if any more dead ladies somehow connected with the Navrones were going to show up in the precinct. When he went into the living room, he was surprised to find Professor August Frye asleep on the couch. He shook him awake.

"I'm leaving."

Frye raised the upper half of his body, got his feet on the floor and was standing in one fluid motion. "I must use your bathroom first."

"You can stay here."

Frye looked around. "Is this your apartment?"

Well, he didn't remember bringing Frye home either so they were even. Frye stepped into his shoes on his way to the john. He seemed to know where it was.

"I'll drop you at your place," he said, when Frye returned, looking fresh, unrumpled, and reasonably clear-eyed.

"Do you realize it is one in the morning?"

"I got a call from Mavis Navrone."

He told Frye about it on the way downstairs. When they were in the car, Frye said, "As long as I'm up, I'll come with you."

Why not? This was an off-duty thing and Frye might be of help with the clearly upset Mavis Navrone.

The doorman didn't know who Mavis Navrone was and Cable couldn't remember the name of the woman Mavis had called about. It was a large building. He told the doorman he didn't want to just ring doorbells until he found the right one.

"My God, I hope not."

"The woman works at Lyndon Johnson Community College."

Pocked cheeks rounded in smiling recognition. "Miss Hangar. That's got to be Miss Hangar."

Mavis answered when Cable pressed the button marked Hangar.

"Thank God!"

"We're an answer to a prayer," he told Frye on the way up in the elevator.

"It is a sobering thought that whatever we do fits precisely into the providential plan. Well, not exactly sobering. That would require coffee as well."

A muffled voice spoke on the other side of the door after he knocked and Cable stepped back so that Mavis could get a good look at him through the peephole. There was the sound of chains being removed. A very frightened Mavis Navrone opened the door but it was August Frye she tugged into the apartment. Cable followed and closed the door, leaving it unchained.

Frye proved to be just the soothing presence Mavis needed, and she told a fairly coherent story while the professor helped her make coffee. Cable just listened in, telling himself he was off duty, it didn't matter that Frye had taken over.

"Phyllis Hangar went to your home in New Rochelle to fetch a portable television?" Frye repeated.

"She doesn't have one here. She never watches it. The radio is PBS and that's it. Not that I'm not grateful to Phyllis for letting me stay."

"When did she leave?"

"Before eight o'clock! I gave her very clear directions, even a map, as well as a plan of the house." She interrupted herself to dial again the number of the house in New Rochelle, letting them hear the unanswered ringing. "She's not there."

Cable imagined her getting mugged in the train coming back. A single woman with as negotiable an item as a television set would be an attractive target. In the meantime, he called into the precinct and asked that New Rochelle be contacted to check out the home of Mavis and Dwayne Navrone, repeating the address as Mavis called it out. There seemed nothing else to do, but Frye and Mavis had settled down at the kitchen table with their coffee. Cable felt increasingly like an intruder.

"Have you spoken with your husband?"

Her mouth opened as if she hadn't even thought of it. Cable called Henny Sheahan's number. Henny sounded the way Cable had felt when he was wakened by Mavis's call.

"Is Dwayne there?"

"Who the hell is this?"

"Your arresting officer."

An audible angry yawn. "Cable?"

"Put Navrone on."

"He's not here."

"Where'd he go?"

"I haven't seen him since morning. I don't think he came back here from work."

Mavis had followed his end of this conversation with widened eyes. "It's starting again, isn't it? It never stopped. They're still trying to get me." She paused and reached out for August Frye's hand. She spoke in a whisper. "What if they thought Phyllis was me?"

2

It was after midnight when Ambrose left the house and walked through the silent streets to the station lot where he had left his car. Strange far-off sounds, the whine and roar of engines, the release of steam, but muted, muted, a nighttime scaled-down version of the day's cacophony. Nearer, the swoop of something feathered, bat or owl, he knew not, but his flesh crept at the sound. The dogs he had heard throughout the night, sitting beside the terrified woman, barked on. She had been limp with fear when he appeared in the bedroom doorway and he bound and gagged her without incident. He might have been returning to Square One, determined to do it right this time, but his intention was not to make up what was wanting in the scheming of Harris, but to bring the man down, flaming across the heavens, like Lucifer falling.

He used the long hours of vigil to rid his mind of all distractions, secondary thoughts, the concerns and demands of his new identity. For now he must close the books on Ambrose Ruffle. He in his innocence had been seduced by the diabolical Harris—this is how he saw it. Against his true will he was enlisted in a deed that had no motive beyond the doing of it.

"We must evolve beyond the notion that our deeds have

any more purpose than the universe itself."

But Ambrose's memory, whatever he might wish, resounded with the psalms that, for so many years, he had daily read. He could think of neither the world nor himself as merely there, a product of chance, going nowhere, meant for nothing. If this was faith he had never lost it.

"You're killing her as a favor to a client," he had said. "That is your purpose."

Harris's smile was ecstatic. "Think of it, Ambrose. Is that me? Philanthropy through misanthropy? Bah. I do it in order to do it."

It. Kill. The woman's eyes never left him, as if she were memorizing every pore in his skin. He had long since removed the stocking which he had worn only to insure invisibility in the night. She could see him plain. It did not matter. Like Ambrose, she was caught up in something and there was only one way out of it. The only way he could get her to close her eyes was to talk to her.

"You've had more than a week of life you might not have had. Of course it was you, not Gloria Sheahan, we meant to kidnap."

This one squirmed and moaned like Gloria. Would she too lose control, wet the bed, drive him from the room?

"You've had a whole extra week."

He almost suggested that she thank God for that. It was important that he not be drawn into his old function as he sat at the bedside of the dying. And this woman was as doomed as the bull who is released into the ring. A ritual must be played out, but the end was inevitable.

So he had settled down and the vigil had been a time of peace and meditation, although there was the annoying interruption of the ringing phone at regular intervals. Of course he did not answer, but the woman on the bed responded to the ringing as to a rescuer. Midnight came.

"I am going for my car. I will be back in fifteen minutes at most."

A guttural growl as he passed a darkened yard unnerved him more than the swoop of presumed bats. A dog. He hated dogs. Barking, snarling, nipping dogs, guarding their turf. This yard was fenced and he quickened his step, the nape of his neck tingling with fear. For a fleeting moment he felt as Mavis Navrone must feel, lying there on her bed, bound, gagged.

3

Cable, Mavis Navrone and August Frye were on their way to New Rochelle minutes after receiving the news that the local police had entered the Navrone house on the instructions of the owner and found a woman tied and gagged in the bedroom.

"That's Phyllis," Mavis said as they dropped streetward in the elevator. "It's got to be Phyllis," she said, when they put her in the back and Frye eased himself with huffing and puffing into the passenger seat. "Thank God, she's alive. They did say she was alive, didn't they?"

Her talking performed some function short of communication. They ignored her. Frye said it had been eons since he'd been to New Rochelle.

"Where's Old Rochelle?"

"In France."

"Why not Holland?"

This set Frye going so Cable drove with a woman babbling in the back seat and a professor lecturing beside him. The guy in the tollbooth didn't even look down at Cable when he took his money. Jack the Ripper could drive all over New York with a sample of his victims and not even be noticed. It was a thought he'd had since dead bodies began showing up in Navrone's back seat.

When they got to the house, Phyllis Hangar sat shivering in a living room chair. Mavis rushed to her, the two women embraced, and began to weep in unison. The locals looked at Cable, and he took the guy in charge into the kitchen.

"What's she say?"

"She came here, went down that hall to the bedroom and the next thing she knew a masked man was in the doorway. We found her gagged and bound, wrists and ankles."

"Sexual assault?"

"She assaulted me when I asked. I guess the answer is no."

"A guy tied her up and left her?"

"He said he was coming back."

"Did he?"

"Not before we got here."

"After?"

An expressionless look. Cable let it go. No point in sounding critical. He didn't know what he himself would have done. From the living room came the soothing voice of August Frye. He had found some brandy and was sharing it with the ladies. Mavis kept asking Phyllis Hangar if she didn't have any idea at all who the man was. She even showed her a photograph of her husband Dwayne.

"Mavis, I don't know. I never saw him before." She shuddered. "I never want to see him again."

At the ringing of the phone, silence fell.

"I'll get it," Cable said. "Mavis, get the kitchen phone and lift it when I lift this one."

4

Getting the drugged Navrone from the office to a consulting room took more of an effort than Harris had been prepared for. Finally, he lay the man on his back, took him by the ankles and unceremoniously dragged him into the pastel consulting room and left him on the floor. He locked the door and returned to the office where he sat at his desk. Outside, Manhattan glittered like a Christmas tree.

He turned away from that infinitely distracting scene. It was possible to be mesmerized by the lights, to stare at closer windows and wonder about the lives being lived suspended there above the street, in a stratum of building, totally dependent on the city's multiple services—water, electricity, heat supplied from elsewhere, everything out of one's control, the very food on which one subsisted brought in daily from beyond the city, from the mainland and neighboring islands. On rooftops one saw areas arranged as if they were lawns at street level, with potted trees and bushes. Perhaps one could grow vegetables and not be totally dependent on others, several tomato plants perhaps.

In Valparaiso, Indiana, where Calvin had been raised, where his father was pastor, city life was not radically different from life in the country. Farmer's wives had their gardens for the household and so did those in town.

Canning in the fall had been a family's way of facing the winter, independent, provided for, ready. People should be closer to God in Manhattan than in Valparaiso. In Valparaiso one nursed the illusion of being self-dependent. In this city everyone was dependent on everyone else. How easy then to imagine one who watched over it all.

Where was Ambrose? It was in such moods that Harris had enjoyed being with his fellow counselor, fellow former Christian, former fellow assassin. They had been friends and now they were enemies. Would Ambrose come for him here?

He lay his hands flat on the desk, bowed his head and cleared his mind. With the going of faith his psychic powers had increased. After five minutes of silence, the phone began to ring in the middle of a ring, which meant the call was being forwarded from his apartment.

"Yes."

"Ambrose."

"I know."

"I have Mavis."

"I have Dwayne."

"What is your plan?"

"To bend with the remover to remove."

"Shakespeare?"

"So you told me."

"What does it mean?"

"Let bygones be bygones?"

"You might have killed me when you shot at me."

"Perhaps I should have."

"Leaving the woman's body in my car could have been worse. How would you have responded when I pointed the finger at you?"

"I never met the woman. I had no idea who she was.

Your automobile would have turned up damning evidence.
I would have had to say very little."

"You killed her."

"And you killed Jennifer."

Ambrose could have a career as an obscene caller,
breathing into the phone as he did. "You're right, Calvin.
Let bygones be bygones."

"Come here and we'll drink to it."

"Should I bring Mavis?"

"Either one of them alive would be capable of embarrassing us both, Ambrose."

"*A bientôt.*"

"*Hasta la vista.*"

The phone was slippery when he put it down. He was
feeling more tension than he realized. Ambrose would think
he had reached him at home. Calvin would prepare an am-
bush for his old friend. But first another call. He dialed
carefully, consulting the note Jennifer had given him. To his
surprise, the phone was answered immediately.

"The Navrone residence." Why did those flat tones suggest a policeman? It could not be the voice of Dwayne;
Ambrose claimed to have the wife.

"Mrs. Navrone, please."

"Who's calling?"

"Harsh. *Daily News.*"

"I'll take a message."

Harris hung up. One thing he was now sure of. Ambrose
had taken Mavis Navrone into custody. Police were not
paying a social call at this hour. Had he killed her? Had he
screwed up again? Either alternative would only serve to
make him more dangerous. Inept but dangerous. Perhaps
more dangerous because of his ineptitude.

Harris wheeled his desk chair into the pastel consulting

room, got behind Navrone and pulled him into the chair, lashing him to it by reversing his belt and running it through the back loops of his trousers and the post of the chair. Behind a picture was the safe in which he kept syringes with which he administered Demerol to patients who found it difficult to confide. Rolling up Navrone's sleeve, he drew back the plunger of an empty needle. He held it dramatically for a moment, thinking of Jennifer, thinking of Gloria, thinking of Navrone's wife who could very well have preceded him into nothingness tonight. Harris found the vein with the fingers of his left hand and then plunged the needle in and brought his thumb and fingers together, pumping nothingness into Navrone's bloodstream.

Then he rolled Dwayne down the hallway, opened Ambrose's office, and wheeled him into place behind the desk. Ambrose's desk chair was an ostentatious one, like that of a Supreme Court justice. Harris wheeled it to his office and turned out the lights. He took the stairway down and, on the second floor, broke open the fire alarm and set it clanging. The lobby was empty when he came into it from the stairs. He went to the book and signed Ambrose Ruffle in at 9:00 p.m. and out at 1:10 a.m.

5

Ambrose was aware that the call he had placed to Harris's apartment had been transferred as the fourth ring began. Presumably Calvin had answered it in his office. Knowing the whereabouts of his nemesis redressed the balance somewhat for his failure in New Rochelle.

When he returned in his car and came along the street on which the Navrones lived, half a dozen police cars were lighting up the neighborhood, some pulled into the driveway, others parked in such a way as to partially block the street. Neighbors had emerged from their houses, and stood in groups of two and three, the women hugging themselves, the men with hands in their pockets, all eyes on the Navrones' house. Ambrose pulled over, got out, put his hands in his pockets and sauntered up to a group.

"What's going on?"

"God only knows. Last week it was a nude blonde in the back seat of his car."

"When did the police get here?"

"They're still coming."

And so they were. Half the New Rochelle force must be on the scene. As Ambrose got closer to the house, he saw a car whose plates indicated it came from Manhattan. Every light in the house was on and he caught a glimpse of Mavis

Navrone. She had escaped twice. Ambrose found he didn't care. She had been Harris's target, not his, and he himself no longer needed her. He leaned against the car and wrote on a page torn from his pocket calendar Calvin Harris's name and the address of his apartment. He opened the passenger door and laid it on the seat. It was like leaving a message in a bottle. Then he went back to his car and got out of there.

In Manhattan he arrived to find a fire truck and sedan parked squarely in front of the entrance of his old office building. When he came into the lobby, the night guard was talking apologetically to a fire chief and several firemen in their fighting rig. Ambrose went to the sign-in book and was startled to see his name already there. He signed in as Calvin Harris, got a distracted nod from the guard as he went to the elevators, and a moment later was being whisked upward.

Coming back to this office after he had ceased being Ambrose Ruffle was unwise. Mrs. Hitters had not removed the Jennifer Bailey file from the cabinet. Ambrose drew it out, and flipped through it. From her very first visit, Calvin had recorded her treatment as if it were being given by Ambrose Ruffle rather than himself. Had Calvin in his black Protestant heart intended to bring down the beast of Rome despite his own secession from the Reform and Ambrose's shaky status as representative of the Church? The aim was quixotic enough to appeal to Calvin.

With the folder in his hand he went into his office, flicked on the light, and stopped like a skater, turning his body to the side. A man sat behind the desk.

"What the hell are you doing in here?"

There was no answer. Ambrose, his flesh prickled with

206

fear, had been backing from the room but now stopped. The office had been dark until he turned on the light. The man was immobile; there was something odd about his eyes. Ambrose edged forward, drawn by the memory of Jennifer. Then he noticed that the chair the man sat in was Calvin's.

The next fifteen minutes were filled with frantic activity. Ambrose wheeled the body into Calvin's office and returned his own chair to his desk. With the office light out so he would not be distracted by the unnerving sightless gaze of the man whose driver's license identified him as Dwayne Navrone, he made use of Calvin's dictating machine, and of Calvin's voice as well. Speaking with the annoying condescension of the astral counselor, he narrated a version of the events of the past week that would greatly simplify the efforts of the police. Speaking as Calvin, he confessed to the murders of Gloria, Jennifer, and Navrone.

"You will notice that I employed the same method in the last two cases. And you will ask why. The answer I give is the answer of a child. Because. I killed these three people because I killed these three people. The deed is self-justifying, as all deeds are. Except perhaps the deed of dictating these remarks—rather than justify myself, I incriminate myself. No, better, I demand credit for what I have done . . ."

Like the note he had left in the Manhattan police car, this dictated message was there to be discovered. Whether or not it would be he left in the hands of . . . Once he would have said the hands of God. He had no adequate substitute now. Jennifer's file he took along.

6

"That was the man who called work and said he'd kidnapped me." Mavis nodded as she spoke, in complete agreement with herself.

"How can you be sure?"

"How could I ever forget?"

Had the same man tied up Phyllis? He had told her he was coming back, but if he did he would have seen that the house was full of people so he called to find out what was going on. Cable once more began to feel the oppressiveness of the neighborhood. Outside, despite the hour, curious natives clustered, their routine again disturbed by goings-on at the Navrones. How could they stand proximity to one another without the luxury of indifference to the ups and downs in others' lives? By the time Cable decided to go, a team of investigators, a dwarfish woman and her beanpole assistant, had arrived to take photographs, dust for prints, and do the thousand other things which once in a blue moon proved to be of some help in figuring out what the hell had happened. New Rochelle squad cars were beginning to disperse; citizens lingered as if they expected an announcement.

The two women got into the back seat; Frye got in beside Cable, pulling a piece of paper out from under him after he got settled.

"You got a light in here?"

"It doesn't work."

As Cable maneuvered out the driveway into the street Frye flicked a cigarette lighter into flame and brought it toward the piece of paper as if he meant to burn it.

"Who is Calvin Harris?"

Cable slammed on the brakes when a squad car unexpectedly backed into the drive in order to execute a turn. The cigarette lighter went out, Frye rocked forward, and in the back seat the two women squealed. Geez. It was good to get out of the drive, out of the neighborhood, and head home in the feeble light of false dawn. The women settled down to confidential whispering to one another, Frye spent half the trip back trying to figure out the seat belts.

"I could have gone through the windshield, James."

"Or vice versa."

"Indeed."

After he gave up on the belt, Frye slept. Cable felt like a goddam cabby. The way he came in, he dropped Frye off first, shaking the professor awake. Frye looked away, confused, but then got oriented.

"Already?"

"Don't look at your watch."

He dropped the women off next, watching them through the door and into the lobby where the night man looked at them with an indifference that endeared him to Cable. If the two women had rolled in nude, the man would have gone back to his crossword puzzle just as quickly. It was five in the morning when Cable fell into bed. And lay there remembering what August Frye had said when he first got into the car. His question pursued Cable into sleep.

Who is Calvin Harris?

7

Not even to friends did Wilfrid describe his job as receptionist to an astral counselor, campy as that might sound. Like many frivolous people, he had a lively sense of his own dignity and he did not often invite laughter or even indulgent smiles at his own expense. Besides, the job, like every job he had held since coming East three years before, was temporary. The only permanent role he saw for himself was as a writer. He had arrived with his box full of manuscripts and a secondhand Packard Bell computer hopeful that physical nearness to publishers would prove an Open Sesame. Long after he had learned the fallacy of this, he consoled himself that he had come where destiny meant him to be. Working in the reception room of the enigmatic Dr. Calvin Harris was merely a passing phase in the unfolding of his life.

"Never lose that sense of just passing through, Wilfrid. It is a prerequisite for mental health."

At first such little pronunciamentos by his employer had impressed Wilfrid. He had written Harris into a short story he was working on, but eventually he decided that Calvin Harris was a fraud. Nonetheless, the clients came in droves.

"That is a feature of the neo-pagan age we have entered upon."

Whatever the hell that meant. Harris had a way of making Wilfrid feel like a clod. From fourth grade onward Wilfrid's folks had been told he was special and he had floated through school on the strength of the promise shown by his test scores. The potential registered by the tests substituted for actually learning anything. For someone who wanted to write, Wilfrid had read very little. He made up for it at work by perusing the patient files. Thus it was that, though there had been nothing more than a cheerful farewell when she arrived, and a little chitchat before she left when he jotted down the time of her appointment on a card and handed it to her, he had felt oddly close to Jennifer Bailey. Her death, the discovery of her nude body in a car in New Rochelle, had struck him as grotesque and plunged him into depression. Harris carried on as if he had not lost a client, let alone another human being toward whom he must have developed some feelings over the period of her treatment.

Wilfrid recognized in Jennifer's recorded hopes and ambitions something of himself, though he fought the notion that his desire to be a writer would go the way of her desire to model. Every weekend he sat for hours at his Packard Bell, sipping Diet Sprite, writing. As often as not, what he wrote was simply the story of his ambition, how he wanted to write, how convinced he was that someday he would sit here at his kitchen table and receive at last the revelation of what it was he was meant to say. He stored these lengthy probings of himself on floppy disks and they resembled the sessions Jennifer had with Harris. He became convinced that eventually the two of them would talk and recognize how alike they were. They would be brother and sister to one another; sex had nothing to do with it. The Jennifer Wilfrid knew was the Jennifer who weekly poured out her soul to the astral counselor. Like himself, she was waiting for something great to happen.

And now she was dead. It was worse than losing a friend, or even a relative. It was like losing himself. He was shocked to find that only half a dozen people showed up for her cremation. Afterward, he walked and walked, the way he had when he first arrived in the city, wondering if it was really worth it. That beautiful young person—whose sensitive psyche he had become privy to, actually copying the tapes of some of her sessions and listening to them on his Walkman as he wandered about in search of things to write about—Jennifer, was dead.

Her tragic affair with Dwayne was the basic theme of her sessions with Harris. Wilfrid felt he had come to know this exploitative lover as well as he knew Jennifer. The life of a counselor was eerie and fascinating, and Wilfrid was in on it. He knew most people only on the surface and was wholly unaware of what went on inside them. With Jennifer it was just the opposite—he had come to know her inside with very little knowledge of her outside. Her beautiful outside. On weekends, when he checked the locks and even closed his bedroom door and experimented with makeup, Wilfrid tried to duplicate in his mirror the lovely face of Jennifer. And now she was gone forever.

He decided that Harris took it a good deal harder than he let on. The doctor had been acting in a queer way for some weeks. Wilfrid associated it with the alliance, if that was the word, with Dr. Ruffle down the hall. The two men consulted one another, made referrals to one another, even provided a second opinion to the other's patients. Harris, who had met patients five days a week and, though he didn't expect Wilfrid to come in, sometimes on Saturday morning as well, began to stay away, to cancel appointments. After the dreadful thing that had happened to Jennifer, Wilfrid wanted to take another look at her file but to his surprise found that it was missing. He was further surprised by the realization that he did not want to discuss its absence with Harris.

For some days now going to work had meant listening to irate patients complain on the phone and often in person about the fact that their appointments had been cancelled. Mrs. Hitters, the lady wrestler, Ruffle's receptionist, was having the same trouble. They talked in a little alcove at the end of the hallway where she went to smoke behind a potted rubber plant.

"I'm a bad influence on those who are trying to quit." There was a deep wrinkle across the bridge of her nose. It looked like a misplaced mouth and Wilfrid pretended that what she said was coming from there.

"I'm just getting out of there." He blew a stream of smoke so thin it was invisible until it blossomed into a cloud about four feet away.

"Your guy away?"

He nodded.

"I think they went off together."

Wilfrid did not comment. Mrs. Hitters was always trying to find out things about him and this might have been a ploy. On the other hand, it was possible. Harris and Ruffle talked by the hour with a rare intensity. Why did they remind him of television evangelists?

In the lobby he chatted with the security guard whose interests were exhausted by the fortunes of the Mets, the Nets, and the Jets but who sometimes expanded his repertoire and remarked upon the weather.

"Your boss spent the night here, I see."

"Come on."

The guard showed him the sign-up book. There was Calvin Harris, big as life, time of entry: 4:02 a.m.

Riding up in the elevator, Wilfrid found himself thinking of excuses for coming in a few minutes late. Weekdays he opened up and had quality time to himself before Harris arrived for his first appointment, which was usually at ten.

The outer office looked as it did on any other day. He switched on the light and then did this and that, making as much noise as he could, glancing at the closed door of the inner office. He sat at his desk and looked at the phone. No light indicated Harris was on the phone. He checked the appointment book. There was to have been an eleven o'clock, but it was one of those Wilfrid had canceled. Whatever had brought Calvin Harris in at the crack of dawn had not been his practice.

Wilfrid settled down at his desk but could not do what he usually did. His Louis L'Amour novel was in the right hand bottom drawer, his Walkman was in the shoulder bag he'd brought from home, there was an el cheapo AM/FM radio, a bank premium, in the desk. He decided he had best not divert himself with any of these. He got up, went to the file and unthinkingly looked for Jennifer's file. Gone of course. He took the next one to his desk, opened it and stared out the door and down the hall where Mrs. Hitters was lighting up behind the rubber plant.

8

The excitement of the night did not alter the habits of age. August Frye could no more sleep in of a morning now than he could run like the fools he passed on the early morning sidewalks. Or who passed him, breathing heavily, gaunt, pallid, eyes starting from their heads, pumping their knees, churning up the sidewalk as if immortality lay at the next intersection.

When James Branch Cable dropped him off he had come inside, sat down before the television in his living room and watched a replay of *The Third Man*. During commercial breaks he first put on coffee, then made toast, poured and drank a glass of cranberry juice, rinsed the dishes, then returned to his chair with his third cup of coffee where he sat thinking of the note he had found in the passenger seat of Cable's police vehicle. The note was in his pocket now. He wished he had removed it before settling down. The next time he went for coffee he would get it out. Not that he had forgotten its legend. Calvin Harris and then a Manhattan address not a million miles from where Frye himself lived.

When he went out for his morning walk, hours before his usual time, he strolled in the direction of the address on the note. He had not gone two blocks when a stick figure in jogging costume called his name. The runner ran in place, grinning like a skull, his shorts flapping at his hips. Frye felt like Dante encountering a Florentine in the lower world.

"Professor! Good morning."

A student? Perhaps. My God, it was Jerome! Frye took him by the hand and led him toward the curb.

"Stop pumping your legs like that."

"I don't want to tighten up."

"Too bad. I was going to suggest the Blarney Stone."

"Now?"

"They have a predawn Unhappy Hour."

Jerome, in the grips of the thought that pounding about the streets in that absurd costume would add one cubit to his stature, put up the semblance of resistance, but minutes later they stood at the bar with glasses of beer and double shots of bourbon before them. Frye tossed off the whiskey and went on telling Jerome of his adventures of the previous night. He brought out the note and lay it on the counter.

"Jennifer Bailey went to him weekly."

"Went to him."

"He is an astral counselor."

"Suffering Lord!"

They had two bumps before they went outside where Frye suggested they go by the address. Jerome insisted on doing some semblance of jogging as they went, but his speed was no greater than Frye's. On the way, Jerome told Frye of the affair between Jennifer and Dwayne Navrone, she now gone to God. And both had been clients of Calvin Harris. The security at the building, when they arrived, was impressive, but Frye wheedled the information that Harris was not at home. For a moment afterward, he stood indecisively outside, Jerome going up and down beside him, then he hailed a cab and, taking Jerome's hand, pulled him inside.

"Tell the driver where Harris's office is."

9

Using a skill a client had taught him, Harris unlocked the door of a parked car across the street from his apartment and settled into the back seat to wait. Throughout the night the traffic continued, thinner but constant, and people walked by, their coming heralded by the volume with which they spoke. Harris felt he was getting a wholly new and not altogether interesting look at the city in which he lived.

He was waiting, of course, for Ambrose Ruffle. But Ambrose did not come. The hours passed, once Harris dozed off, but a glance at his watch told him that, incredibly, he had been asleep no more than fifteen seconds. His eyes had grown used to such darkness as the thoroughfare had known but gradually that began to lift, the streetlights went out, a different sort of passerby appeared. It seemed inescapable that Ambrose was not coming.

Of the dozens of possible explanations of his not showing up, Harris began to consider the vagueness of their agreement to meet. "Here," he had said, meaning his apartment, although he had been speaking from his office. The call had been automatically tripped from the phone in his apartment on the fourth ring. He was certain he had never mentioned this to Ambrose. Then he was uncertain. He imagined Ambrose waiting for him at the office and ruminating in an analogous way.

His plan here had been to hail Ambrose before he went into the building, to persuade him to drive again to the cottage near Morristown, to write finis to their friendship and then to let the police close their books on Ambrose Ruffle, indecisive serial killer who could only stop himself from killing by killing himself. Meeting Ambrose at the office would be very different. Particularly when Ambrose saw who was seated at his desk.

Harris put himself in Ambrose's place. Either he would not have found Dwayne and, wondering where Harris was, would go through much the same thought process Harris himself had. But he would phone the apartment and get no answer. He would get no answer either there or at the office when the call was automatically transferred. It seemed time to scrub the plan and get some sleep.

But just as he sat forward to unlock the door of the car, he saw the strange couple stop across the street. An elderly man with wild white hair on the sides of his head and a high domed baldness on top with a jogger who seemed unable to come to a full stop. They went into the building and Harris eased back in the seat. He could make them out, chatting to the guard. A few minutes later, they came outside and almost immediately went off in a cab. Strange. Why did he think they had come looking for him?

He was distracted by the appearance of a man wearing a derby beside the car. Next to him was a policeman. The man unlocked the door but the cop opened it and looked in.

"Get out of there. On this side."

Harris was at a complete loss for words. He stepped out of the car, a smile on his face, hoping for inspiration, but before he could speak, the cop had snapped handcuffs on his wrists. Harris tried to pull away but the cop gave a sharp yank on the cuffed wrist, which pulled Harris toward him. He was off balance when the other cuff was snapped on.

"You got to come and swear a complaint," the officer said to the owner, who had stooped over to examine the inside of his car. Did he imagine Harris had dirtied it in some way? Still bent over, the man looked at the cop.

"You saw for yourself that he had broken into my car."

"You gotta make the complaint."

"Now?" He looked at his watch, tipping his head back to get it into the right lens. "I can't now."

"Then I'll have to let him go."

The owner looked again into the back seat, then made an impatient noise. "Oh, let him go. But you should run him out of the neighborhood."

"This is my neighborhood," Harris said, confidence returning. "Officer, I want that man's name."

"Ask him."

"I have a car identical to this one. I was waiting for my driver." He turned sideways and shot a hip at the cop. "Take out my wallet and check my identification."

"I have to go." The owner adjusted his derby.

"Wait a minute," the cop said, and released Harris from the cuffs. "Now show me your identification."

He studied what Harris handed him, then said to the derby, "He lives right across the street."

"I don't care where he lives, he was sitting in my car."

"I shall sue you for false arrest," Harris said, addressing the derby. "Officer, check his identification."

The falling out between his adversaries was complete. They were still discussing the matter when Harris left them, cutting across the street.

"He's jaywalking," he heard the derby cry. "Look at him. He's jaywalking."

He got safely across and into his own building where he asked the guard what the little old man and jogger had wanted.

"They asked if you were in."

"Did they?"

"I figured I could tell them you was out since you was out."

Harris left this uncommented on.

He emerged from the elevator on his floor and was almost to his door when he heard a noise behind him. He started to turn but saw nothing before the plastic bag was pulled down over his head, over his shoulders, over his arms, and he was pushed forward. He hit the floor and almost simultaneously was struck on the head and a deeper darkness descended.

10

There was still no sound from the inner office and Wilfrid considered just breezing in as if he didn't know Harris was there but he vetoed that almost before he formulated it. Rule number one, Harris had told him when he hired him, is never interrupt a session, never knock on or open a closed door. Rule number two is: always keep Rule number one. Harris smiled grimly as if he thought that was original, but Wilfrid got the picture. Counseling was a confidential business. To interrupt would break the spell as surely as interference from the audience in the theater. Harris had not restricted the rule about closed doors to the doors of the consulting rooms.

He had been behind his desk an hour and it was driving him nuts. Mrs. Hitters went down to the rubber tree for her second smoke of the morning and he went to talk to her, his heels clacking with satisfying authority as he marched down the marble hall.

"Why don't you smoke at your desk when Ruffle's on vacation?"

"Who says he's on vacation?"

"Is he in? Is he seeing patients?"

"Even so."

Wilfrid bummed a cigarette. He hadn't smoked at his

desk either when Harris had been erratic coming to the office, but that was the point. He might show up at any time. Harris himself smoked but the unstated rule was that Wilfrid was not supposed to smoke.

"I cite you as an example of someone who has overcome the habit, Wilfrid. A chain-smoking receptionist sends all the wrong signals."

Smoke signals? He put the question to Harris in imagination when he ran through the exchange at home. In that same conversation, he pointed out to Harris that he himself smoked and the smell of tobacco clung to his clothes. In imaginary conversations, he spoke with careless ease to his employer. At work he was afraid of him. Physically afraid. Harris had mean eyes.

The elevator opened and an elderly man came out and looked to left and right. He was followed by a skinny dude in sweats.

"Get a load," Mrs. Hitters said.

The old man heard her, and shuffled toward them. "Where's Dr. Calvin Harris's office?"

"Do you have an appointment?" Wilfrid asked frostily. Harris's patients needed help but these two looked as if they had escaped from the funny farm.

"Come, professor," the thin one said. "It must be this way."

His tennies made obscene sounds on the marble floor as he went down the hall. The old man followed him.

"Hey, wait," Wilfrid said. "I'll show you." Professor? "I work for Dr. Harris. Wait."

They ignored him. He'd be damned if he wanted them going into the office when he wasn't there so he picked up the pace, went past them and put on the brakes, sliding up to the door of the office. He rounded the desk and got into his chair before they came through the door.

"Harris in?" the professor asked.

Wilfrid flipped open the appointment book and covered the empty page with his hand. "Name?"

"Is he in?"

"Yes."

The old man sauntered to the closed door and, before Wilfrid could stop him, opened the door. The skinny guy in shorts got there before Wilfrid did. The three of them stood in the doorway, looking at the man seated at Harris's desk.

"He's dead," the old man said.

"That's not Dr. Harris!" Wilfrid pushed past the old man but once in the office he stopped. The dead man's stare seemed to be on him.

"Who is he?" the old man asked.

"I don't know!"

"Jerome, call Cable."

"Here he is!"

11

Cable had called Frye to ask why the professor had mentioned Calvin Harris and, when Frye did not answer,
looked Harris up and decided to stop by the man's office.
What exactly he would say when he got there he left to inspiration, dumb luck, or the citizen's willingness to volunteer information to the police. When he arrived, he found
Jerome Jarbro in what looked like his underwear, August
Frye red-eyed and glad to see him, and a nervous Nelly
named Wilfrid who kept saying he didn't know who the
dead man sitting at Harris's desk was.

"Dwayne Navrone," Cable said. He stood in front of the
desk looking at the corpse.

"Dwayne Navrone?" the twit said. "He's a patient. He's
been here before."

Cable shooed everybody out of the office then left himself, closing the door. He used the phone on Wilfrid's desk
to summon the medical examiner over here.

"I'm going home and change," Jerome said as if he'd just
noticed he was running around town in that skimpy costume.

"I think I'll stay," Frye said.

Wilfrid, the receptionist, was eager to talk about his day
thus far, how he had arrived to find the door of the inner of-

fice shut and of course he hadn't dared open it.

"Why'd you think he was in there?"

"The book downstairs. He'd signed in very early in the morning."

Cable made sure that book was secured and taken into custody by the men who were arriving in response to his call. Winston came in whistling and waggled his brows at Wilfrid, who looked at the medical examiner in horror.

"Where?"

"The inner office."

Winston, followed by two assistants toting equipment, disappeared into the inner office. Frye returned from examining the consulting rooms.

"Don't lose your mind, James. This place would drive you nuts."

"Remember last night when we left the house in New Rochelle?"

"Vividly."

"Why did you mention Calvin Harris?"

"Because of this." He produced a piece of paper and handed it to Cable. "It was on the seat of your car. I sat on it."

Wilfrid was sitting at his desk and had been joined by a woman who had a lighted cigarette cupped in her hand. Cable put the paper in front of Wilfrid.

"That the doctor's handwriting?"

He lowered his face toward it, keeping his hands on the seat of his chair. But it was the woman who spoke.

"That's Dr. Ruffle's hand!"

12

Ambrose lay the bagged and now bound Calvin Harris on a couch in the living room of Harris's apartment. He pulled a chair up next to the couch and addressed the plastic bag.

"Now you know how that woman felt, Calvin."

No answer. Ambrose turned, picked up a glass ashtray from the coffee table, and rapped Harris on the head. The plastic bag turned violently away and Harris wedged his head into a corner of the couch, in the angle of the arm and back.

"Can you see anything, Calvin?"

"Don't try to be sadistic, Ambrose. It's just not you."

"You're right. Sit up."

After a moment's hesitation Calvin rocked himself into a sitting position. Ambrose gave him another sharp rap on the head with the ashtray.

"Goddamn that, cut it out."

"The last person I saw trussed up the way you are ended up dead. You killed her."

"And you killed Jennifer."

"No, you did. You also killed Dwayne Navrone in the same way and made the mistake of propping him up behind my desk. I put his body where it belongs, behind your desk."

Silence behind the plastic bag and then a movement perhaps produced by Harris's nodding. "Ambrose, I congratulate you. I sought to place the sole blame for our ventures on you; you have found me out and sought to direct attention solely to me. Am I correct?"

"Not just sought. I have succeeded."

"There I cannot agree with you. We are both guilty of the same error, Ambrose. We shall hang together or we shall hang separately. I suggest that we call a truce, consider our best individual interests, and join forces to insure that neither of us can suffer for what we have done. You say you put Navrone's body behind my desk?"

"I deny your premise, Calvin."

"Ah, the eternal Scholastic."

"Unlike yourself, I run no risk of punishment for having allowed you to involve me in your nihilistic misdeeds."

"Jennifer. Remember Jennifer, Ambrose. That was your work."

"What you don't realize, Calvin, is that I have already ceased to be Ambrose."

Ambrose stood and went into the kitchen. Behind him, Calvin called, "Where are you going? Wait, don't go."

Ambrose returned with a steak knife, pinched the plastic between his fingers and punctured it with the point of the knife. Then he tore the plastic bag away from Calvin, who came blinking into the light. Ambrose realized he would be silhouetted against the window behind him. He moved back and forth in front of Calvin, enjoying the other man's astonishment.

"Who are you?"

"The voice is the voice of Jacob but I have become Esau."

Any doubt he may have had of the transformation he had

effected in his appearance in recent days was removed by Calvin's reaction.

"Ambrose?"

He spoke as he had when Calvin was enclosed in the plastic bag. "Of course I shall change my mode of speaking as well. Ambrose Ruffle has ceased to be. And now Calvin Harris will cease to be."

He lifted the knife, enjoying the way Calvin's eyes stayed with the moving blade. He let it drop. From an inside pocket of his suit jacket he drew a case, opened it and took out a hypodermic needle.

"You shall die as Jennifer and Dwayne did, but in your case, the injection will be made in such a way that it will seem self-inflicted. It will be thought that, overcome with remorse, you killed yourself as you did those two."

He did not yet act, however, unable to master the impulse to squeeze all the vindictive satisfaction from the moment. Calvin's condescending manner was utterly gone, his expression was one of fear, terrified fear, he could not tear his eyes from the hypodermic that Ambrose flourished. Both men froze when the bell rang.

"Thank God they've arrived," cried Calvin, trying to raise himself from the couch. Ambrose pushed him back.

"Who?"

"Answer the door and find out." His old manner was back and Ambrose was unnerved. He could do what he had planned and plunge the needle into Calvin's vein and depress the plunger, forcing lethal oxygen into his bloodstream. But the bell rang again and there was the pounding on the panel as well.

"Come in," shouted Calvin. "Come in, come in."

"Shut up."

Ambrose ran back to the kitchen. There was a door there

which when opened gave onto a back stairway. He started down it. He would just leave. Calvin had seen what he now looked like, but Calvin would have far too much to answer for to interest the police in chasing him.

He stopped counting the floors as he fled downward, stopping only to listen for sounds of pursuit, but there were none. He continued down to the basement of the building, went out the service door into an alley and moments later was on the street. He walked slowly past the building, noting the police car at the curb, continued on until he disappeared into the crowd.

Part 5

GOING, GOING, GONE

1

Calvin Harris was a pleasure to listen to, at least the first several times. The astral counselor was only too happy to tell James Branch Cable how the demented Ambrose Ruffle had killed three people and been in process of killing a fourth.

"Thank God you arrived in time."

"Amen," purred August Frye, who had asked to sit in. It would have been churlish to deny the old professor access to these sessions given the role he had played in events that may indeed have saved Calvin Harris's life.

"Why would he want to kill you?"

Harris smiled as teachers smile on pet students. "I consider myself relieved of the obligation of confidentiality."

According to Harris, he and Ruffle had been patients of one another.

"A counselor has a professional duty to detect the onset of neurosis before it impedes his ability to help others."

"Is killing people a neurosis?"

"In Ruffle's case, emphatically not. True, he would count for mad by ordinary canons. He considered himself a Nietzschean *übermensch*." Harris included Frye in his smile. "He killed in order to assert his independence of any moral code that would limit his freedom."

"Who was his accomplice?" Cable asked. His voice was phlegmatic. He had been proceeding on the assumption that he was in pursuit of one murderer and that Calvin Harris was his man. But Harris, in telling of the kidnapping of Gloria, spoke of two men lurking on the stairway.

"Me!" Harris lay the tips of his fingers on his chest and with raised eyebrows looked back and forth between Cable and Frye. "Can you believe it? I was told we were to take custody of a violent patient. Unorthodox, yes. But there are times when unusual methods are required. Imagine my surprise when Ambrose pulled a plastic bag over her head. I have to admit it was an effective device. And then we set out for New Jersey."

Harris led them to the cottage near Morristown and the locals swarmed over the place with Winston and company in the thick of the hunt. There was little doubt that Harris had led them to the site of Gloria's murder. Would he have done that if he were not the innocent dupe he claimed?

"I was far away when the murder occurred, of course, having slipped away in Ambrose's car."

"How did the body end up in Manhattan?"

"I can only tell you what Ambrose told me."

The story was corroborated by findings of New Jersey police. A taxi driver told of the fare he had taken to the Newark Airport.

"When did you first realize he had killed the woman?"

"The following morning."

"And you didn't call the police."

"I felt checkmated, Lieutenant. He had bamboozled me into accompanying him. Doubtless you will find fingerprints of mine in the New Jersey cottage. By putting the poor woman's body in the car of a patient of mine, he made speaking up even riskier. Furthermore, he confided these things to me, lying on a couch in my consulting room. It would have entailed overcoming my professional persona to tell the police what I had heard from a patient."

"Surely he wasn't a patient in the usual sense," Frye asked.

"Confidentiality is a seamless garment."

"You have a doctorate?"

"Yes."

"In astral counseling?"

"In theology."

This fascinated Frye, and Cable left the two to make a visit to the men's room. As far as he was concerned, Harris's degree was in bullshit. The Ambrose Ruffle to whom he attributed the murders was nowhere to be found. For all Cable knew, he was lying dead somewhere, the fourth victim of Harris's calculated spree. Later, he developed his theory for Frye.

"The only 'oobermensch' I see is Harris. He's the one who decided to kill a lot of people for the fun of it. Now he's having more fun telling me stories about how the other guy did it, the guy we can't find."

"His fingerprints were found in New Jersey too."

Prints that matched those found all over Ruffle's office and apartment.

"So where is he?"

"On Harris's story, he took off before you entered the apartment and found Harris bagged and bound."

"Harris is sly as the devil."

"Sly! He certainly is. He puts the corpse of one of his patients in a car in New Rochelle . . ."

"We have only the word of Wilfrid that she was a patient. There is no record of her seeing Harris."

"Why would the man's receptionist lie?"

"A lover scorned. You heard Harris."

"It was also very sly to prop another dead body up behind his desk after thoughtfully leaving his calling card on the seat of your car."

"Do you think Harris is innocent?"

"Not at all. He has a degree in theology."

"Be serious."

"I think they were in it together," Professor Frye said. "I think he was left holding the bag. Or vice versa."

Cable was relieved to hear that. Not that he had hesitated to ask the prosecutor to proceed against Calvin Harris. If they didn't have enough to put Harris away, he was a monkey's uncle. Or vice versa.

Mrs. Hitters indignantly dismissed the suggestion that her employer had anything to do with the murders.

"Dr. Harris was a bad influence on him. I always thought that. But Dr. Ruffle was so sure he could bring the man around."

"Around from what?"

Mrs. Hitters frowned at August Frye. "Are you a policeman?"

"Around from what?" Cable repeated. He didn't want Frye saying he had not seriously pursued every stupid remark. Mrs. Hitters didn't know. But she knew Harris had been a bad influence on Ambrose Ruffle.

"Has he been in touch with you?"

"No!"

"Where do you think he is?"

"That you'll have to ask Dr. Harris."

2

Indictments were brought in, a trial date was set, and Cable
was taken up with other things, though whenever they got
together August Frye sooner or later found himself bringing
up the case of Calvin Harris.

"Any luck finding Ambrose Ruffle?"

"No body has turned up."

"Oh, he must be still alive."

Believing Harris selectively was hard to justify, but Frye
found the assumption that Harris had bagged and tied himself and waited to be discovered wholly incredible. When,
after he had nagged James for weeks and Winston had lifted
fingerprints matching those all over Ruffle's office from the
knob of the back door of Harris's apartment, the result was
dismissed.

"Harris says they were friends. He says Ruffle visited
him in his apartment many times."

"Leaving by the back door?"

"August, what's the point if we can't find the man?"

It was the fact that Harris had a degree in theology and
that Ruffle, if Harris could be believed, was a flown priest
that clinched Frye's interest. Harris had told Frye this almost casually when James made one of his frequent trips to
the restroom during the extended interrogation. Cable, de-

spite his relative youth, had the bladder of a Richelieu.

"Diocesan?" Frye asked Harris.

"Oh I'm sure."

"What diocese?"

"One of the upstate ones."

To make up for Cable's disinterest in this, Frye checked the Catholic directory. No Ambrose Ruffle, but then the man had gone over the wall. But there was no Ambrose Ruffle in the previous twenty years of the directory.

"I think Ruffle was an assumed name," Harris said.

Harris's smooth reaction to the results of Frye's research suggested the agility of the habitual liar. Frye wavered. If it had not been for the fact of Ruffle's office, the undeniable presence of Mrs. Hitters, and fingerprints in New Jersey, in the offices down the hall from Harris's and in Harris's apartment, this absent accomplice might have seemed only a product of Harris's imaginative effort to exonerate himself.

"Perhaps he lied to you," Frye suggested.

"He did little else. But not on this. There is no doubt that he was a priest."

"Was?"

"Ah, you know the Catholic belief. If once, then always."

But Frye had wondered if Harris was referring to Ambrose Ruffle in the past tense.

He went along when Cable showed Zolar, the prosecutor, around the relevant locales of the case. They ended in Harris's apartment where Frye wandered musingly into the kitchen, opened and closed, then opened again the back door. He went through it and pulled it shut behind him. The lock clicked. He turned the knob, pushed, repeated the process, and realized he had locked himself out. He knocked on the panel and waited. Apparently neither Cable nor Zolar heard. He waited. He turned and considered the stairway down which Ambrose Ruffle must have gone. Frye started down.

By the time he regretted having begun the descent, he was too far down to go back. Behind was Mount Everest, ahead was the tedious but less demanding if endless flight of stairs. Did anyone ever use them? The thought that Ambrose Ruffle might have been the last to do so perked him up and, as he went down, he searched the stairway for some telltale object. He imagined Ruffle dropping his wallet or a monogrammed handkerchief or . . . anything. The wild possibility made the descent tolerable and before he realized it he had come to the door that gave onto the lobby. He hesitated. The stairs continued down. If Ambrose Ruffle had emerged into the lobby on that fateful day he might have been seen by the gathering constabulary. August Frye continued down to the garage.

He stood in the great echoing chamber, half filled with vehicles. A ramp led up to sunlight and the street. Frye moved slowly among the cars, shuffled up the ramp and stood on the walk outside. The row of taxis parked along the curb set his mind going.

"Sure I'll make the inquiry," Cable said patiently after they had parted from Zolar and were ensconced in a Blarney Stone with strong drink on the table before them. Frye had called up to Harris's apartment to let Cable know he was in the lobby. "I wondered where you went."

"Once I started down I couldn't stop. It's the way Ruffle must have gone."

Cable sipped from his glass. He listened to Frye's belief that the fleeing Ambrose Ruffle had hopped into a cab at the stand just outside the garage of Harris's building. He agreed to have the matter investigated. Frye wished he would show a modicum of interest in the chance of locating Ruffle.

"If we find him it will be a separate case. Zolar's success with Harris will be crucial."

In short, Ambrose Ruffle was a mere footnote to a case Cable considered all but closed. Nor did the data provided by the cabbies seem helpful. Two had taken male fares from the cab stand at the appropriate time and a third had taken a woman. Other cabbies had arrived at the cab stand too long after the time that Ruffle would have emerged to warrant inquiry. Had Ruffle been either of the two men who had taken a cab from that stand within twenty minutes after Harris had been discovered bagged and bound upstairs?

"Twenty minutes?"

"Go down those back stairs some time."

One driver had taken his fare to Wall Street, the other, Fusad, had been directed to Sutton Place. One afternoon, Frye wandered about the East Side and came to where Fusad had dropped off his fare. St. Luke's stood on the northwest corner of the intersection. He sought Fusad out and had a muddy coffee in a restaurant whose spicy air made breathing seem a prelude to Pepto-Bismol. The driver's freshly shaven face seemed as they talked to be in the process of producing its beard.

"Hey, this was how long ago? You tell me I took a guy from there to Sutton Place, okay, I did. The records say so. That don't mean I remember doing it."

Do drivers notice who gets into and out of their cabs? A moment's reflection should have told him how unlikely it would be that Fusad should remember. Besides, there was Harris's unsettling remark that he had not at first recognized the Ruffle who had attacked him in his apartment.

"He had altered his appearance completely. Even his voice."

Cable just looked at Frye. It was difficult to quarrel with James's intention to see Harris as the sufficient solution to those three murders. The elusive Ambrose Ruffle would add nothing to the solution.

"If he wasn't victim number four."

Sitting in the courtroom when Calvin Harris went to trial, August Frye was struck by the absence of media attention, but then what are three murders among so many? The spectators that did gather seemed jaded before the jury was selected; they whispered, read books, might just as well have been on a park bench outside. If I had ever committed a murder, Frye told himself, I would have expected the attention of the world, myself the cynosure of every eye, daily business suspended until the drama played itself out. But being tried for murder, like being born or dying, went on without disturbing the even tenor of the city's ways.

On the third day it occurred to him that the well-groomed man in the blazer and striped tie had not missed a session. He bet himself the blazer would not be there the next day. He won the bet, but then the next day was Saturday. On Monday morning, however, moments after the judge entered the blazer slipped in and took a seat. August Frye was at the very back and able consequently to study in profile this faithful attendant at the murder trial of Calvin Harris.

The man seemed aware that he was being watched, and Frye directed his gaze toward the front of the courtroom where the elegant bench and jury box were bathed in dusty sunlight that fought its way through the unwashed windows. A plan formed in Frye's mind as he fought a sense of excitement. He would get word to Harris, ask him to survey the courtroom unobtrusively. Was the man in the blue blazer and today solid tie the absconded Ambrose Ruffle? Hadn't Harris described the transformed Ruffle as dressed like the interested spectator?

A recess came and Frye started toward the defense table but then stopped when the blazer left the room. Had he been frightened off by Frye's staring? Frye hurried into the corridor and nearly bowled over the blazer who was lighting a cigarette.

"I need a smoke," Frye said apologetically, invoking the camaraderie that exists among the remnant of confirmed smokers.

The man in the blazer nodded.

"Could I borrow your matches?"

The blazer handed the book over.

"Dominus vobiscum," Frye said.

"Et cum spiritu . . ." The man stopped.

As if he had not heard, Frye struck a match. The man drifted away as Frye held the lighted match in one hand and patted his pockets with the other. No cigarettes. He blew out the match just as it began to roast his fingers and slipped the matchbook into the pocket of his tweed jacket. The man in the blazer continued on down the echoing corridor, not fast, not slow. Was he leaving? Frye felt pulled in two directions. The matchbook suggested a Solomonian solution.

3

Were there court scenes in Dante's *Inferno?* James Branch
Cable had wasted two days waiting to be called by Zolar.
Winston was on the stand and loving it and so was the defense. Winston seemed obsessed with the idea that we can
know nothing for certain. The exchange between him and
the defense attorney recalled drunken barracks conversations in which the possibility that life was a dream had been
covered like a blanket. The recess did not help. He hurried
to the men's room where he had to wait for a urinal. Were
there public restroom scenes in the *"Purgatorio?"* Back in
his seat behind Zolar, Cable turned when he was nudged.

"Take this," August Frye whispered, pressing something
into Cable's hand. "And don't smudge it! Check it for
prints."

Frye went away, doubled over in order to be unobtru-
sive, and Cable palmed the matchbook and put it into his
pocket. Many people Frye's age were well along into Alzhei-
mer's. How fast does the mind go? Cable felt his might go
at any minute. Winston was making an epistemological
point and Zolar groaned.

"The sonofabitch is my witness."

"Never trust a chiropractor."

Zolar turned and stared at Cable. "Chiropractor?" Zolar

repeated the word silently, a syllable at a time, as if he were about to spell it.

"I meant brain surgeon."

Zolar returned to the agony of the cross-examination.

Cable was on the stand for the rest of the day, reading from his notebook, fending off the fallacious parries of the defense, ignoring Calvin Harris who seemed to be asleep. Several times, Cable put his hand into his pocket but withdrew it suddenly when he felt the matchbook. Where the hell had August got it? Frye was not among the spectators, and Cable found he half resented not having his old professor see him in an official capacity.

"Any idea what we're looking for?"

"You'll know," Cable said, and Winston decided to be flattered by the remark. "First thing in the morning."

"What's your rush?"

"You want me to do it now?"

"I wish I could tell you the importance of this."

Cable wished he knew if it were important or not. When court adjourned, August was nowhere in sight. Winston said he would do it himself and immediately. Cable went to the men's room, wondered if he should go to the precinct and await Winston's results there, decided to wait. He had spent all day waiting and was getting good at it. He took out a cigarette and found he had no matches.

He had fallen asleep in his chair. Winston was standing in front of him, nodding with satisfaction.

"They're the same all right. Cable, we have a dozen samples of the same prints. They all belong to the guy you call Ambrose."

"The ones on the matchbook too?"

"Yup. Where did you get it?"

"I wish I could tell you."

Not a very friendly way to express his thanks to Winston, but Cable was anxious to find August Frye and find out where he had gotten hold of that matchbook.

Frye was not at home, he was not in his office, he was not at the one or two bars close to home and office that he frequented. Cable found it impossible not to wonder where the old professor was. The matchbook made it clear that he had located Ambrose Ruffle, identifying him in what might be the only possible way if Harris was not exaggerating the transformation in his erstwhile colleague. Cable brooded over his dinner and felt no inclination to linger in a bar. At home was the threat of television but if he didn't turn it on at all he was safe. He settled down with Dante, intent on finding the answers to the questions that had occurred to him in the courthouse.

4

After leaving the matchbook with Cable, August Frye left the courtroom and went down the corridor in the direction the man in the blazer had taken. Outside, he stood on the top of the steps and looked up and down the street.

"Looking for me?"

He turned to face the man in the blazer. "Ambrose Ruffle?"

The man's expression altered, tenseness giving way to a relieved smile. "I thought so."

"I will not say you've changed, since I never knew you in your previous incarnation. But, after listening to Calvin Harris, I feel I know you."

"Who are you?"

"Professor August Frye."

"How does Harris concern you?"

"In a way you might describe as purely *per accidens*."

"You have a weakness for Latin."

"And in it. I suppose you couldn't lose yours."

"What has Calvin told you?"

"Everything."

"Do you drink?"

"When I'm not asleep."

Ambrose laughed heartily and took Frye's arm as they

went down the long flight of stairs to the sidewalk. Ambrose asked if there was any place nearby August would recommend.

"This isn't my neighborhood."

"Nor mine. Shall we take a cab to the Plaza?"

"The Plaza! Wonderful."

Twenty minutes later they were seated at a table, able to see and be seen, Frye with a Manhattan, Ambrose with a glass of mineral water.

"When were you ordained?"

"I want to talk about Calvin Harris, not myself."

"Your loyalty is touching. I refer of course to your daily attendance at your friend's ordeal. He insists that you should be in the dock with him."

"Poor fellow."

"He says that it was you who killed the two women as well as Dwayne Navrone. Your disappearance lends credence to the charge."

"He threatened to implicate me. That is why I disappeared."

"How much do you know?"

"Of Calvin's exploits? Only what he told me."

"He said you drove him to New Jersey and killed Gloria there."

"I was in my apartment when that must have happened."

They spent several hours reviewing the matters for which Calvin Harris was on trial. Ambrose told a preposterous story, as preposterous as Calvin Harris's when he had argued that Ambrose was solely responsible for the three murders. It seemed clear to August Frye that the two had been in it together. When Frye pushed back from the table, saying he must visit the restroom, Ambrose too got up.

"Good idea."

The waiter fluttered and they decided to pay up and go on. Frye pressed into the cashier's hand a note he had scribbled surreptitiously on a napkin as they talked. He linked his arm in Ambrose's and sauntered toward the street exit. But he turned and caught the cashier's eye and nodded.

"Where to?"

"Have you ever been to the Blarney Stone?"

In the cab, August Frye made a ceremony out of giving instructions to the driver. The man obviously wondered why they were going so far when there were any number of the chain bars along the way.

"The Plaza is not what it was," August Frye said loudly, sinking back just as the cab shot forward.

He gave the cabby directions and they were let off on the Upper East Side.

Things were different in his neighborhood Blarney Stone; he felt more in control.

"Stay with mineral water," he advised Ambrose. "Never mix your drinks."

"The stuff is diuretic."

"You'll find what you require down that hall."

While Ambrose was away, Frye dissolved half a dozen Valium tablets in the ex-priest's mineral water. They sank down through the ice cubes, sending bubbles to the surface presided over by a wedge of lemon. He told the waiter to contact James Branch Cable at the precinct.

"What for?"

"He'll want to know where I am."

The man had gone grudgingly away before Ambrose returned. They touched glasses and drank deeply.

5

August Frye was in scarcely better shape than his companion when James Branch Cable arrived at the Blarney Stone. He had been to the Plaza, he had been in the process of checking cabs, calling the precinct to do so and then was told of the message from the Blarney Stone. August and the man in the blazer were leaning toward one another, singing Gregorian chant to the fascination of disgruntled Catholics at neighboring tables.

"Why did they get rid of that?" a red faced man demanded of Cable. He meant the music. Cable pulled up a chair.

"James, this is Ambrose Ruffle."

The man extended a hand. Cable took it firmly and with his other hand snapped a cuff on it. There was a small struggle before he got the other wrist manacled. Ambrose Ruffle was weak as a noodle and his speech was slurred.

"I'm surprised he's still awake, James."

"What's he drinking?"

"Valium, mainly."

And Ambrose, looking at his manacled hands, began to nod. His head fell forward. Cable put in a call to the precinct. Two officers were there in minutes.

"Take him away," Cable said, indicating the sleeping Ambrose.

"What's the charge?"

"Public drunkenness. And first degree murder. I'll be there in a minute."

But first he wanted to get August Frye out of the bar and home where he belonged.

"He's guilty as sin, James."

"Who isn't?"

"Oh, he'll love talking to you."